Love

Inc

Love Inc

SHUCHI KAPOOR

Srishti
PUBLISHERS & DISTRIBUTORS

SRISHTI PUBLISHERS & DISTRIBUTORS
Registered Office: N-16, C.R. Park
New Delhi – 110 019
Corporate Office: 212A, Peacock Lane
Shahpur Jat, New Delhi – 110 049
editorial@srishtipublishers.com

First published by
Srishti Publishers & Distributors in 2018

Printed at Repro Knowledgecast Limited, Thane

For my mother –
my teacher, my friend, my everything.
I am who I am because of you.

Acknowledgements

This book wouldn't be possible without the unflinching support of Arup and his amazing team at Srishti Publishers. Thank you, you are the best!

Heartfelt appreciation to my favourite critics – Amrita and Deb, Mansi and Prashant, for your invaluable feedback and infinite patience. A special mention to Maneet, whose faith in me surpassed mine.

A big shout out to Sapna, my fairy godmother, for solving all my Earth related dilemmas.

Hugs and more to Ansh and Aadya for letting their mother escape to her dreamworld more often than not.

And finally, words aren't enough for the man who makes my world go around. Thank you Anuj for this incredibly surreal journey. You are the wind beneath my wings!

Incessant rains seem welcome only in Bollywood movies, where drenched people are sexy and not bedraggled or stinky. Landing at the Chhatrapati Shivaji airport at Mumbai, Gayatri got her first flavour of these much touted July rains. Needless to say, she had come ill-prepared for them, focussed only on her upcoming job interview at JBCN Corp. Her morning flight from Delhi had taken off on time and she thought she was well within her set time schedule. But the weather looked set to play spoilsport as she headed towards the prestigious Nariman Point in a 1950s fiat taxi, the hinges of which threatened to come off any minute!

This interview was extremely important to Gayatri and her love life. Nakul, the centre of this love, worked in Mumbai with the renowned HMM Ltd. He had landed the job during campus placements at BMS, the top b-school in Delhi where the two had met. With the passing of time, the distance between Noida and Mumbai was becoming a bit much, both in kilometres and hearts.

Gayatri stood at five feet with clear, almost luminous skin, jet black straight hair and expressive eyes. A gregarious persona, with childlike laughter bubbling out of her most of the time, she was opinionated and naïve in equal measures.

While not exactly her anti-thesis, Nakul would best be described as average looking with a forgettable face and a shy personality. With a lanky frame on a five feet eight inches tall body, he would probably escape one's notice at first, except if someone were to catch him making a presentation or addressing any issue close to his heart. Their classmates were surprised initially when Gayatri and Nakul started dating, but very few people actually knew that she was captivated with guys who were natural leaders, possessing high IQs and a wicked sense of humour. All of which Nakul had, along with a sense of calm that he brought to her hyperactive personality. While for him, she was simply the brightest star in the galaxy, who, by some great stroke of luck, had landed in his small world.

The affair which had started almost three years ago had the makings of turning into something permanent. Nakul had decided that she was 'the' girl, and had been insisting on her finding employment in Mumbai.

Gayatri was currently employed at an IT firm as part of the human resources team, at Noida, also her hometown. Her journey from womb to work had been accomplished well within the borders of the 'northern delights of India'.

Nakul's call jarred her out of the reverie. "Hey babe, where have you reached?"

"Had you come to pick me up, you wouldn't have needed to ask me this," retorted Gayatri sarcastically.

He sighed, "You know I would have been there had it not been for this last minute presentation."

"Have reached Worli, shouldn't take more than twenty minutes," she finally replied.

Swivelling his face away from the 40th slide on the PPT, Nakul tried to explain the topography of Mumbai to her; the fact that Andheri West was on the other side of the city, at least an hour away during peak traffic hours, which had already begun.

Gayatri disconnected the call after extracting a promise from Nakul to meet at some point during the day, before she caught her flight back at seven that evening. Her conversation with the job consultant had Gayatri ready to meet the HR head. If she cleared this round, she would have to come back to meet Mr Kapoor, the company chairman. She speculated that Mr Kapoor was the type who insisted on being part of the day to day functioning of the company. Going by his track record though, he may be forgiven any eccentricities.

JBCN was his latest venture in a string of hugely successful companies. Consulting and solution providing was a normal practice, but what set JBCN apart was that it promised the entire package of setting up the company for the client. For example, if XYZ approached JBCN with a proposal of wanting to start a company, JBCN would convert itself into XYZ for those 6-12 months, where it would source finance for the company, hire personnel, set up procedures, oversee site build-up and function as XYZ till its teething problems were weeded out. Post this, the client would be hand held and slowly complete charge would be handed back to the client. This was the first time something like this was being attempted in India and though the company was in its nascent stages, it was already creating a buzz in the country. It also made the roles of all personnel in JBCN extremely fluid and challenging at the same time, not to mention chaotic. And Gayatri just loved chaos…in fact, thrived on it.

She wasn't aware of the intricate details, but on the whole, the concept appealed to her high energy personality. There was also a disquieting rumour doing the rounds that it was actually the son, Kapoor Jr who was the brain behind this company, but knowing whatever little that she did about him, Gayatri had her doubts. At thirty, he was the poster boy for rich daddy's indulged, if not spoilt, son.

"As one of the biggest business houses, the least he can do is upgrade the look of this ancient looking office building," she muttered as she stepped down from the cab. As with most Mumbai buildings, the archaic structure did not prepare her for the opulence that met her eyes once she entered the place. The words that immediately came to her mind were plush and elegant. Muted hues ruled the upholstery and her surroundings. There was character and an old charm to the place, which Gayatri appreciated. Always having considered herself to be born in the wrong century, she loved everything about the 18th century Victorian era. She proclaimed herself to be the biggest fan of Jane Austen and Charlotte Bronte, and greatly appreciated subtlety. Of course, that didn't stop her from practicing flamboyance and embracing everything modern.

Approaching the receptionist, she stated her appointment and was asked to wait. She sank into one of the mammoth couches while her mind went back to the ongoing conversations between her and Nakul for the past few months. The long and erratic working hours for both of them weren't giving them any time to Skype or FaceTime, let alone meet. Since Nakul's job with HMM was his dream, it was up to her to try and seek employment in the same city as him. This did mean staying away from her parents for the first time in twenty-three years, but hey…it was all for love!

After waiting for about a quarter of an hour, Gayatri walked up to the receptionist to get a status check on her interview.

The hassled looking woman looked up and said, "Something urgent just came up which requires Mr Mishra's immediate attention. This would probably take an hour or so."

With Nakul still in his presentation, there was nothing for Gayatri to do except leaf through the many corporate magazines scattered around in the lounge. Rohit Kapoor, fair and tall, was an extremely good-looking man, despite his age. As per gossip columns, tennis and his wife's strict ministrations kept him fit and energetic. Gayatri hoped that she would be reporting to him and not his son, who seemed to be the frivolous kind, lacking ambition and drive.

She dialled her mother to give an update on the current goings-on. In her case, 'my mother is my best friend' was the truth and Mrs Neena Vohra knew almost all that there was to know about her daughter, including her relation with Nakul. He had had to pass the litmus test with Mrs Vohra. Privately, Mrs Vohra was still not convinced that he was the right guy for her daughter.

The receptionist, Darla, brought Gayatri back from her musings. "Please take the elevator and go to level 4. Someone would be there to meet you."

Grateful for some action finally, she took a detour to the washroom, stopping to freshen up and check her appearance before reaching the elevators.

She walked out on the fourth floor and was directed to the cabin of Mr Sudhir Mishra, the HR head. After exchanging pleasantries, Gayatri was quizzed about the latest HR practices and her grasp of the same.

After a couple of hours into the interview, Sudhir said, "Now that I have understood a little about you, let me tell you something about our company. JBCN is synonymous with a work force which adapts itself to new projects, ideas and people within a very short period of time, over and over again. This means we have to employ people who are extremely high on positive energy, bordering on over-confidence. It's great to have such people managing projects, but when it comes to managing them, it's any HR team's nightmare."

He took off his horn-rimmed glasses and continued, "Hence the need to bring in personnel who can handle unexpected things along with chaos and sift through all the irrelevant information to identify and tackle the real problem. My question to you is – are you that person?"

Gayatri replied with a smile, "All through my formative years, I was chided for my craving for pandemonium in and around my daily life. So the one thing I can promise you is that I perform much better when dealing with the unexpected."

She continued in her enthusiasm about the company, "Despite managing such a huge empire, Mr Kapoor has managed to innovate and evolve. This speaks volumes about his vision."

Sudhir frowned and replied, "Oh, you seem to be referring to Sr Kapoor. This project was Aaryan's brainchild and he has been extremely passionate and hands-on about it. He has been adamant about getting the right HR person in place...you are the eighth candidate we have interviewed in this month."

It was 3.30 in the afternoon when she finally got out of Sudhir's office and was asked to wait while her future in JBCN was pondered over. Exhausted, she sat down in the company cafeteria. Her phone rang.

"Where have you been, why aren't you taking my calls or replying to my messages?" asked Nakul, sounding a touch worried.

"It's been hectic and this is the first normal breath I have taken in the past couple of hours," she retorted between mouthfuls of not so-bad food.

"I am still awaiting the verdict and will tell you everything once I know it myself. How did your presentation go? What time are you reaching here?" In her usual style, she bombarded Nakul with her queries rather than answering his.

He grinned into the phone, "Only if you allow me to talk, my love, would I be able to tell you that I have already reached Nariman Point and am waiting outside your building."

Just then, the peon came to tell Gayatri that they were ready for her upstairs. She hurriedly disconnected the call with the assurance to keep him updated and headed towards the elevators.

Reaching Sudhir's cabin, she knocked and was asked to take a seat.

He began, "I really like what I have observed in you, Gayatri, and would like to take this further by introducing you to our MD, Mr Kapoor. So if I ask you to postpone your tickets from today evening to tomorrow morning, would that be a problem?"

Gayatri was pretty sure she would be able to manage it at her current workplace and nodded.

Upon reaching the lobby, she realised that this time, they were taking the elevator marked 'Private'. In no time they had reached the head honcho's office, or rather his lair. While the whole building could be described as stylish and neutral, this floor screamed alpha male – whether it was the sleek furniture or the brooding greys and blacks on the decor or the expensive looking portraits, leaving no one in doubt that one had arrived at the lion's den!

As Sudhir informed the secretary of their arrival, Gayatri's edgy nerves started screaming danger for no explainable reason. Walking into the room with her feet sinking into the absolutely decadent carpet, she got her first look at the man or rather his profile, since he was talking on the phone and had his back to them. Her eyes feasted on toned muscles stretching the pink striped shirt tucked into a tapered waist and her gaze had to travel a long way down to take in the grey pants with shiny black shoes.

As he turned around, finishing his call, Gayatri revised her opinion about him. This was a sleek panther rather than a lion. Chiselled cheekbones and arrogant eyebrows clashed with the unfairly long lashes which concealed the expression or the lack of it in his eyes. The thin sensuous lips and a George Clooney cleft defined the strong jaw line. She realised that while her surreptitious scrutiny was going on, Mr Heir Apparent had subjected her to a toe to head appraisal as well.

Having heard praises about her quick thinking and confidence from Sudhir, Aaryan was looking forward to meeting a seasoned, professional lady. Instead, he saw red painted nails peeping out of wedged heels (ugh, he hated wedged shoes on women!), fitted pants and a crumpled shirt covering some eh... not so bad curves!

With a scrubbed face, devoid of make-up and a pig-tail, she looked like some school girl playing grown up. What was Sudhir thinking? Yet, respecting the man's judgement, Aaryan asked them to be seated.

Before he could start the questioning though, Gayatri rushed ahead and said, "If I may be bold enough sir, you have a fairly well designed program to assess potential candidates…"

Aaryan sat back in his chair and thought resignedly, here comes the gushing flattery.

He was used to it ever since he had attained his looks and position. He indicated her to continue.

"But don't you think it is inadequate or rather incomplete as a tool?" she finished a touch breathlessly.

For a silent minute, Aaryan didn't think he had heard correctly. *She* was trying to question his methods?!

Controlling his irritation, Aaryan said evenly, "And why do you think that, Ms err…Vohra? Have you reached this conclusion from your vast previous experience?"

Ignoring his sarcasm, Gayatri said, "Only if you allow me to finish, Mr Kapoor, my point is also precisely this – if a novice like me could assess the gap in the evaluation system, then it definitely needs sprucing up. Maybe you need to add a few more curve balls to the game, maybe like some simulation exercises."

Sudhir tried to cover his smile with a discreet cough. Aaryan was thoroughly peeved, but only for a moment. He revised his original assumptions about Gayatri and took her seriously for the first time since she had walked in. After thirty minutes of intense grilling, which revised Gayatri's opinion about Kapoor Jr. as well,

Aaryan finally relented and agreed with Sudhir's decision… for now.

Aaryan leaned back in his chair and said, "Ms Vohra, we make quick decisions at this office. So here is the offer: Thirty percent hike from your current salary base and accommodation to be provided by the company, but joining within the fortnight and three months' probation period, failing which, you would be terminated with immediate effect. If you are okay with these basic conditions, Sudhir can take you through the details."

Without waiting for her reply, Aaryan buzzed his assistant for his next appointment to be sent in.

Gayatri told Sudhir that the termination clause sounded a little harsh and she would revert to him by the next morning. Agreeing that it had been a long day, they set up the meeting for the next day at 10 a.m. She was impatient to see Nakul, who'd been waiting outside for her all this while.

Half an hour post that interview, Aaryan headed out of office for a meeting. It was the new hire, Ms Vohra, gesturing wildly at someone across the street from the office porch. Then without any regard for oncoming traffic, she ran onto the street, barely making it to the other side in one piece.

"Does she not have any common sense? I sincerely hope that I have made the right decision in hiring her," he muttered.

With these uncharitable thoughts about her, Aaryan saw her running into someone's arms, nearly crushing the poor guy in the process.

The guy wouldn't be complaining though.She is definitely worth a look with those hazel eyes and wide smiling mouth. But too short and curvy for my taste, thought Aaryan.

Not that I am interested or anything, he added hastily in his mind.

Oblivious to anything else, Gayatri was blabbering away to Nakul about the day's events while he simply soaked her in.

"Take a deep breath first and tell me what you've eaten till now,"said Nakul.

Irritated at being interrupted for such mundane things, Gayatri glowered at him and said, "I don't remember!"

"Aha, which means, we are hungry since this morning! Now I won't hear anything till you sit down and eat something," said Nakul.

They hailed a cab and went to Kala Ghoda, an area known for its mouth-watering eateries.

"You will forget your favourite kathi rolls after eating a chicken roll here," Nakul boasted.

Surveying the dimly lit area, Gayatri took her first bite of the much praised roll.

Rolling her eyes, she exclaimed, "Your taste buds have turned to dust, if you think this puny sized roll can come even close to the ones back home."

Nakul burst out laughing at his girl's theatrics and her blind love for anything north. He himself had barely passed muster as he belonged to Madhya Pradesh.

Thinking back to the first time he had seen her at the b-school, clad in a bright kurti and leggings with her lustrous hair swinging with the breeze, he had felt as if someone rammed into his solar plexus.

"That is Gayatri," his friend Amar had said after seeing Nakul open-mouthed for five minutes.

After completing electrical engineering together and four years of working experience, they had been selected in the same management program at BMS.

Not to be found wanting in counselling his friend, Amar had said, "A girl that pretty would surely have a boyfriend hanging around. Even if that's not the case, she would definitely be high-maintenance."

Not that Nakul could hear or register anything his friend was blabbering. He just couldn't get enough of looking at this girl.

Nakul turned around to Amar, "What did you say her name is?"

Thus began Nakul's manoeuvres to try and see Gayatri at least once a day. This required considerable effort, since she was part of a different course and was a day scholar. It would be six months before a 'marketing fest' would bring them face to face for the first time. Nakul, though normally reticent, was a fantastic orator and hence a natural choice for making presentations in front of any audience. And so, on day one of the fest, Gayatri saw this guy captivating everyone in the auditorium with his oratory skills. By the time it ended, Gayatri realised that average height and looks and a non-descript hairstyle hid an extremely intelligent mind and a keen sense of humour.

As everyone started to leave the auditorium, she walked up to him and introduced herself, "Hi, I am Gayatri, first year HR. You were fabulous up there."And with that, she offered her hand.

Sensations which couldn't be described were running through Nakul's entire being, but he stood frozen. Taking his lack of reaction as a snub, Gayatri turned to walk away.

"Just for your information, it has been 4320 hours since I first saw you," said Nakul to her retreating back.

Gayatri spun around in surprise.

Nakul's eyes blazed with intensity as he said, "And to be

honest, you have lived in my head for most of those hours. Can you suggest a cure?"

She didn't know how to respond to such ardour and couldn't stop the blush spreading furiously all over her face. She muttered something about having to go for a class and walked away.

It still amazed Nakul how he had mustered courage to say all those lines to her on that fateful day. Bringing his head out of the past, he listened as Gayatri described her 'long' day at JBCN corp.

"I think you should take up the offer and give it your best for the first one month. You will get a fair idea as to whether it's working for you or not. If not, then we would still have two months to find you another job in the city," Nakul finished pragmatically.

Gayatri always took his advice seriously as far as career decisions were concerned. With her head more in the clouds, it was usually Nakul who steered her away from emotional decisions. Listening to him, she decided to give JBCN and Mumbai a try.

The company was putting Gayatri up at The Ambassador Hotel located on Marine Drive for the night.

As they reached the hotel entrance, Gayatri pouted, "Tell me again why you can't stay here tonight. If I can come all the way to meet you from Noida, the least you can do is spend the maximum time possible with me."

"Sweetheart, you know I would have if I could. More than you, I am the one dying to spend some quality time with you," he declared passionately.

"But this Singaporean team is creating havoc for me at

work. I have to be in office by 8 a.m. and I didn't even carry a change of clothes with me. In a fortnight, you are going to be back here and then hopefully every evening together..." Nakul cajoled her.

Bidding him goodnight, Gayatri went up to the room and caught up with her parents on FaceTime. After showing them the view from her hotel room and giving a detailed account of her day, she went off to bed, dreaming about sleek panthers.

The next morning, Gayatri communicated her decision to join the company, and then headed straight to the airport. She went directly to her current office and gave in her notice. She had to use all her charms on the grumbling but good-natured boss for an early release instead of the customary one month. Reaching home, Gayatri grew nostalgic as she stood at the house's threshold thinking about her departure in a few days.

As the only child of her parents, Gayatri had been fairly pampered, though not spoilt, and the thought of her leaving and going away, was making her parents anxious. A fairly successful businessman, Raj Vohra was a self-made person and valued honesty and perseverance above anything else. While he was the bread earner in the house, Neena Vohra was the foundation on which their household ran. Had Gayatri wished, she could have chosen to take a cushy position in her father's mid-sized business. But both her parents had encouraged her to find her own space as an individual and a professional.

A merit student herself, she had tried to raise her daughter with a strong value system and all the freedom that she herself hadn't been accorded in her times. Mrs Vohra had passed on not only her intelligence but also her good looks to Gayatri. With her husband's humour trickling through her daughter, all in all, Gayatri was Neena's biggest accomplishment.

As a modern mother, she did try to support her daughter's relationship with Nakul, appreciating the honesty which both the kids afforded her. Neena just wished that Gayatri would give it a little more time before fully committing herself to it. Her problem was not with Nakul. To her, Gayatri seemed more in awe of his qualities than in love with him.

Helping her pack and prepare for Mumbai, she reflected upon the conversation between Raj and herself the night before. "I am not sure if her decision to move to Mumbai at this stage of her career and life is wise," said Neena.

"Normally I would agree with you on this, but I have full faith in that boy. Nakul Shrivastava is a very sensible person with a mature head on his shoulders, though it's a shame he is a vegetarian," laughed Raj.

"Can we have any conversation without food cropping up," asked an irritated Neena, "and he may be sensible, but our Gattu isn't always so," she retorted.

"In her limited exposure to the world, Nakul is probably the smartest guy she has encountered. What if that were to change tomorrow, not to mention the fact that Nakul's mother openly dislikes Gayatri," she finished.

Countering her, Raj said, "I believe he offsets her beautifully and if life holds any other plans for Gattu, then she has us to advise and support her in whatever she chooses to do. Now stop worrying so much and get me another katori of that wonderful moongdal halwa."

Shaking her head, she looked at Gayatri who was trying to

make a list of things to be packed or discarded or stored. Sighing, she decided that this wasn't the right time to speak on the topic and got on with the task at hand. Finally the d-day arrived and with a little trepidation and some tears, Gayatri left for Mumbai, to what she hoped was going to be the best phase of her life.

This time, her Nakul was there at the airport. He had taken an off from work to get Gayatri settled in before her big day. The company had provided accommodation for her at a building in Colaba, where a lot of JBCN's other employees also stayed. Getting off from yet another ratty taxi, Gayatri looked up at her new lodging with growing horror. The feeling notched up instead of dissipating as she entered the dubious lift to go to her cramped 1BHK. Shutting her nose against the onslaught of the 'fishy' smell, she surveyed her apartment. Cramped was an understatement. The low ceiling bathroom seemed to have been forced upon the flat, instead of being part of the original structure. But before she could verbalise her thoughts, Nakul rushed in to assure her that his lodgings were way worse than hers.

"Considering my housemaid's quarters are better than this back home, I am not sure how you can convince me otherwise," fumed Gayatri.

"Trust me, this is one of the posh localities in Mumbai. Wait till you see mine," grimaced Nakul.

Not willing to stay another minute in the flat, irrespective of what her boyfriend said, she dumped her belongings and told Nakul to show her some local sights. Happily, he played the local tour guide. Eventually, it was the proximity of a shopping place to her lodging that endeared her flat a little to Gayatri.

After a hearty lunch at Leopold and his narration of its infamous history, she sighed, "I guess I need to start unpacking and settling in."

Knowing her very well, Nakul asked her to go ahead to the flat, while he shopped for some basic supplies and groceries. By the time he came back to her flat, the sun was setting. Gayatri had somehow managed to spread her exuberance in her flat. There was a bright red spread on the bed and an indigo bowl for knick-knacks on her kitchen counter and various memorabilia across the place. The place looked cheerful and sparkling already, just like his life with her presence in it!

"What is the point of me living in the same city as you, if we can't even share the flat? How much time would we be able to give each other like this?"questioned Gayatri.

"Till we are not sure that this is the company that you will be with, I don't think we should move from our respective lodgings. Let's take a call on this in another three months, once you complete your probation," said Nakul.

"Must you be so logical all the time? What happened to romance and love directing our decisions," demanded Gayatri, and before he could reply, held up her hand and said, "I know, it's all for our future; don't need to hear it all again."

Nakul grabbed her, entwining his fingers through her hair, inhaling her perfumed skin, letting it take over his senses.

"Do you know how intoxicating your smell is?" he breathed.

"It's the Body Shop scrub effect. You should try it too," she replied impishly, moving away from him.

As he tried to catch hold of her again, his phone rang. He

turned away to take the call.

Nakul came back and said, "I have to go back earlier than I thought. There are some changes to that Singapore project report which I have to incorporate tonight itself."

Gayatri replied evenly, "It's okay love, but when will this blasted project finally get over?"

He sighed and said, "I don't know, but it's extremely important that I don't screw up this project as it can put me on the fast track with the company. You know that I am not great at inter-personal skills, no? These days networking is more important than one's actual work."

Gayatri wrapped her arms around his skinny midriff and assured him, "They'll be blind not to appreciate your work or recognise your worth. So forget all the nonsense about what is the norm, just concentrate on what you do best!"

After Nakul left, Gayatri tidied up whatever there was to do in the playhouse sized flat and decided to call it an early night.

Dressed in a knee-length, pencil black skirt with her customary white shirt, Gayatri felt a mix of nervousness and excitement as she stepped into the JBCN building the next morning. Darla, the receptionist, welcomed her warmly and handed over the orientation program details. She introduced her to Taruna, who worked as one of the project managers. Both women wished Gayatri all the luck for her first day.

Gayatri grinned back at such a warm welcome and went to report in for the orientation, with a promise to catch up later. There were five people who were joining in with her; everyone in operations, except herself. During the next three days, they were taken through the exact workings of the organization and interacted with most of the business heads. But the best was the interaction with Sr Kapoor, one of the most brilliant minds she had ever encountered. To top it, he was very affable and approachable. Gayatri wondered if the son was adopted, since his interaction was to the point, almost bordering on curtness.

Mulling over her boss's temperament, Gayatri almost missed hearing about the party that night, marking the end of their orientation period. Attendance was a must for all six of them and Gayatri rushed home, her mind on the million dollar question – what to wear? Thankfully the party was at Taj Colaba, a few minutes by cab from her place, which gave her enough time to at least wash her hair and put on some make-up. She chose to wear a midnight blue dress, with a cowl neck and decided to leave her now shining hair open. Some sparkly eye shadow and a pale pink lipstick finished the look. She sent her dressed-up selfie to Nakul before she left for the hotel. Gayatri was really looking forward to the evening. She loved parties, especially the dancing kinds!

Aaryan tugged at his office tie, standing in the private suite on his floor as he waited for his assistant to get the spare clothes. He didn't enjoy such office gatherings, especially the part about having to remain sober since he was the boss(!). These parties usually wrapped up with him playing the agony aunt for most of his staff. Contrary to his carefully constructed image of being a hard ass, Aaryan was a big softie and often ended up using his heart over his head in a lot of matters. He believed that this had aided him reaching where he was today, winning him undying loyalty of a lot of good guys in the process. Nonetheless, it *was* a draining exercise and not one that he was looking forward to, more so, on a Friday night.

He reached the hotel lobby only to be reminded about the short conference call by his ever efficient assistant. He found himself a quiet spot next to the pillar while he logged into the call. Suddenly his eyes fell on the delicious confection in killer heels and a mid-thigh blue dress. It took his astonished mind a few seconds to realise that the 'confection' was actually his HR... the company HR; he amended hastily in his head. Partially hidden behind the pillar, he renewed his perusal of her from head-to-toe and back again.

"This is not appropriate attire for an office party," he muttered to himself, without realising that he was still logged into the conf call!

AK apologised for his mutterings and wrapped up the call a couple of minutes later. Wordlessly, he followed Gayatri as she found her way to the party hall, registering every smile she bestowed. Was she blind to all the leers that she was receiving, stupid girl?

"And why am I getting bothered by it, anyway?" he mumbled.

Gayatri entered the hall greeted by loud thumping music. The party seemed to be in full swing already. After she completed the formalities of greeting Sudhir and other senior colleagues at the bar counter, she went to join her contemporaries on the dance floor.

"Boss is in an exceptionally bad mood tonight," said Dhruv, coming up to Gayatri and her gang of newbies.

He was one of the many managers that Taruna had introduced Gayatri to.

"You mean AK? Call me AK, everyone in office does,"

repeated Abhay, imitating Aaryan.

"Isn't he always in a bad mood?" countered Gayatri. "Why would you talk to him during a party? Don't you get enough exposure during the week as is?" she continued.

Saying so, she turned around, finding herself face-to-face with the topic of their conversation. At his raised his eyebrow, she blushed furiously.

But he simply asked, "Are you all here for a meeting or to dance?"

Relieved at not having been caught, she gave him a dazzling smile which he took as an acceptance to dance with him. Aaryan took her hand as they started matching steps to a popular English track.

Gayatri was aware of the close proximity to her boss. Strangely, her lungs found themselves short of oxygen and her head a bit tizzy. She could feel the warm imprints of his hands everywhere he touched her and her senses were getting the onslaught of the yummilicious smell of his cologne. Looking up, she found him staring at her.

Though the song wound up, Aaryan was loathed to let her go. It was Gayatri who took an unwitting step back and he dropped his hands immediately.

She faked nonchalance she was far from feeling and went to join some other office girls on the dance floor. Though she didn't turn around, Gayatri could feel AK's eyes boring into her back.

Aaryan discovered that there was something wrong with the liquor that night. A couple of drinks were making him feel close to the edge and decidedly out of control. Though a tiny part of his brain told him that maybe it was the saucy minx on the dance floor who was responsible for the same.

Why am I thinking about her at all? She is my employee and *I do not* mix business with pleasure ever. After the stern lecture to self, Aaryan decided to walk out of the party and go elsewhere.

Gayatri got dropped off at her flat by her newly-formed friends, Taruna and Sujoy. She changed and got ready for bed, but found herself too restless to sleep. Punching her pillows for the umpteenth time, she gave herself a strict talk about the lure of bad boys and arrogant bosses and told herself to be absolutely professional henceforth.

She settled into a good rhythm at work and realised that JBCN was a fairly well-oiled organization. AK believed in a hands-on approach and was completely transparent and accessible during work hours. Things were totally professional yet pleasant between them and AK deserved the credit for it. Nakul and she managed to spend enough quality time together, at least on the weekends. Her mother had visited the city the previous week and they had enjoyed visiting most of the famous sites. Finding her daughter a little thinner and less radiant, she had cooked and stocked up enough food to last her a fortnight. Life, Gayatri decided, was good!

It was the third month of her probation and by now, she had begun to love the organization. Even the city was growing on her.

"What's the latest gossip, Darla?" asked Gayatri the next morning.

Darla was the hub of office grapevine and though Gayatri didn't indulge in office politics, sometimes it was fun to know what people were up to.

Darla beckoned her close and whispered, "AK's girlfriend is

back. What will happen to all the crushes floating around in the office? They'll get crushed," she giggled at her own play of words.

"I didn't know he had a secret lady tucked away," said an intrigued Gayatri. She loved affairs and their complexities and of course happy endings.

"Huh, what do you think? A hunk like him won't have a steady girl, and what a girl? She is in his cabin now and they have been enclosed there for an hour now. Wonder what they are up to," winked Darla.

Gayatri went upto her cubicle, her thoughts on the mysterious lady in AK's cabin.

Right then, Taruna rang on the office line, "The managers want to know today's menu."

"At this rate, I should start charging you all; the amount of cooking I am doing is parallel to a dhaba these days," Gayatri grumbled.

"At least let me start my work for the day and tell the boys to hold onto their tummies. It's a surprise," she said with a smile in her voice.

The necessity to eat good food was the propeller of experimenting in the kitchen for Gayatri. The unpalatable food at the office café and the dabba at home made her develop new skillsets in her minuscule kitchenette (aided by Mrs Vohra's instructions on the phone). The end result was a gradually improving lunch box, its success being denoted by the frequent raids on it.

Aaryan's day at office had started normally but unravelled pretty fast. First the latest client created new guidelines at the last minute. Then, AK's long time on and off girlfriend, Devika decided to land directly from London into his office.

"I have decided to quit my job and relocate to India. Dad wants me to settle down and frankly, I am bored of Europe too. By the way, I called your mum from the airport and she was ecstatic to hear the news," said Devika, without pausing for a breath.

"So what say you? Ready to get shackled this year, Mister twelfth most eligible bachelor of Mumbai," she finished, referring to a magazine survey done the year before.

Aaryan was stumped! He was totally clueless about how to respond to her. He pushed her out of the office citing an important meeting, with a promise to catch up with her at dinner. Taking two stairs at a time, he reached the fourth floor, to find it nearly empty. When the peon informed him of the reason for their collective absence, he went down to the cafe. And his irritation soared to new unparalleled heights. Ms Siren Vohra was holding court, with all his, apparently besotted managers fawning all over her. After being ignored for full two minutes, he cleared his throat to gain everyone's attention.

Sujoy spoke with his mouth full, "AK, you gotta try this rajma chawal…straight from the heart of Punjab."

"I am sure! Thanks, but no thanks," said Aaryan, barely holding onto his temper. 'Ms Vohra, please see me in my office, once your, err, luncheon is over," said he through gritted teeth.

Why has the 'saddu boss' version resurfaced? wondered Gayatri after he left.

Apparently everyone else also sensed that there was something amiss and the remaining food was consumed faster, almost in near silence.

Gayatri went upto AK's now familiar lair.

"You wanted to see me, AK?" she enquired.

Much calmer now, he launched into the new hiring requirements as had been requisitioned by the client.

Leaning back into his throne, he asked, "So are you running a parallel kitchen to the cafe down below?"

"Err… it's a newly discovered hobby, one I am enjoying and sharing with my friends," she replied coolly.

AK enjoyed watching the play of expressions on Gayatri's face. Most days it didn't require much effort. Today wasn't any different and she had already adopted her militant stance.

He realised that he enjoyed their on-going banter. With a sudden brainwave, he uttered gravely, "Now that you are here, we might as well discuss your performance in the past three months."

"But the period doesn't finish till the end of this week," Gayatri squeaked, caught totally unprepared.

"I don't see how that should make a difference," he replied in all seriousness.

"So, let's get Sudhir into the conference room next door and wrap this up now," Aaryan finished.

With her heart pounding, she ran to her cabin to get some relevant printouts. Straightening her fuchsia pink kurta, matched to a white Patiala salwar, Gayatri squared her shoulders and walked up to the conference room. She entered the room, finding both men already seated and in the middle of a serious discussion. Her heart sank at the looks on their faces.

"I should have behaved more soberly and portrayed myself a little more maturely, less…" chiding herself mentally, she nearly didn't realise when Sudhir started to address her.

Severely, he said, "I am sure you can figure out what we are going to say to you and I think our decision is fair."

"But won't I be allowed to give my version in this?" asked Gayatri, a touch nervously.

"I don't think it's required, Ms Vohra," said Aaryan in his trademark deep voice.

Sudhir started to speak, but Gayatri interrupted him, "But I like working here and am ready to work upon whatever shortcomings there are."

Sudhir shook his head and replied, "I am afraid our decision is quite final – we simply cannot let you go *away*. So please sign the permanent employee contract kept in front of you."

Gayatri realised she had been had by these scoundrels.

"'You have nothing better to do with your time, except torture your unsuspecting employees!" she spluttered, forgetting that she was addressing her superiors.

Both men burst out laughing, causing her to glare at them. But being a good sport, she joined in reluctantly.

"Now stop lingering around, wasting our time. We have more people to, what was the word, eh, torture," said Aaryan and shook her hands warmly.

A thrill ran through Gayatri's body, which had nothing to do with her new 'permanent' job status.

"When he smiles, he more than makes up for all that grumpy behaviour. The looks, the smells, the IQ… shit, I've got to stay away from him," she swore quietly.

Skipping back to her workstation, she called up her mum and gave her the good news, including the theatrics.

"This boss of yours sounds quite interesting. You never did tell me how he looks," said Neena Vohra mischievously.

"Do not even think about matchmaking, Mom. You know

my emotions are engaged elsewhere," said Gayatri.

"My darling girl, I asked a simple question. It's your Freudian mind which is trying to read more into it," countered her Psychology Hons. mother.

She called Nakul next and asked him to join her for a celebratory dinner that night.

"But it's a weekday, Gayatri. I promise we'll celebrate your success with a big bang on this coming Saturday."

"Why can't you move away from your schedule once for us? It's a big day for me and I am going to celebrate, with or without you," saying so, she banged the phone down.

Nakul went back to work, dismissing Gayatri's theatrics. Work had always been paramount to him and he didn't like disruptions. He knew that Gayatri was going to sulk for a couple of days, but he also knew exactly what was needed to get her back in good humour.

She was put out by Nakul's unenthusiastic response. He hadn't even called back to make up with her. Boyfriend available or not, she decided to celebrate. Armed with her favourite *Pride and Prejudice*, clad in her favourite, almost threadbare shorts and tee, she awaited her favourite meal from a nearby Chinese restaurant. Right on cue, the doorbell rang and she opened the door with the wallet in her hands, only to find the most amazing bunch of white and pink lilies in a sparkling cut glass vase. On the card it was signed 'JBCN'.

She placed the vase carefully on the kitchen platform and immediately messaged Sudhir, *Thank you for the most amazing flowers.*

Sudhir called back within a few minutes, reprimanding her

for sending messages meant for someone else to him. Gayatri realised that there could be only one other person who would have sent her these. Suddenly feeling inexplicably shy, she sent a simple 'Thank you' to AK. Sitting at a five-star hotel, listening to Devika go on and on about their future plans, Aaryan smiled at the message, thinking, 'at least someone is happy tonight'.

After checking her phone for the umpteenth time, Gayatri finally called it a night, put off slightly by no communication from either Nakul or AK. Though she couldn't describe any reason for the disappointment due to the latter.

Driving Devika home in his Porche two-seater, Aaryan mused over his conversation with his soon to-be-fiancée. For the past two hours, he had tried to explain to Devika that his near future plans didn't include any kind of romantic attachment and JBCN was his prime focus. But to his dismay, Devika turned out to be more cunning and a better negotiator than he had given her credit for. She assured him that she didn't want to get married anytime soon, nor had any intentions of interfering in his fantastic business plans.

Devika had purred, "Honey, I only want us to be together. I am willing to wait for you as long as you like. Maybe just an intimate family gathering to share our intentions towards each other, hmm? Think how happy your mother will be about this."

Always a sucker for emotions, Aaryan couldn't think of any possible way to back out of such a proposal and he promised to speak with his parents about it. After a lingering kiss, Devika got out from the car, reminding him of his promise.

Situated at the prestigious Malabar Hill, home held no appeal for him that night. As the security ushered his car in through the gilded ornate gates, Aaryan left it at the porch to climb up the marble steps into the palatial double storeyed lobby. Similar to all their offices across the country, the Kapoor house was done in muted colours and understated elegance, highlighting the architect in his mother. A highly sought after interior designer, Mrs Anjali Kapoor, was a force to reckon with – both outside and at home. As Aaryan asked the staff to inform his mother of his arrival, he was told that she awaited him at the rooftop poolside.

His mother had stopped waiting up for him since the age of thirteen and Aaryan wondered if something was amiss. He took the lift to reach the bar counter near the pool and hugged her.

"Is everything alright? Why are you up so late?"

She tweaked his nose and replied, "Devika called me and informed me of your momentous decision. I didn't know you were looking to get married."

"Yeah, that makes the two of us," grimaced her son.

Mrs Kapoor made her only child sit on the bar stool and gave him a look… the kind that makes one want to vomit out everything to her.

"Tell me what is bothering you," she said calmly.

Aaryan, only too happy to oblige, launched into a detailed account of her visit to the office and the following dinner.

"I can handle the affairs and the liaisons, Mom, but all this serious stuff makes me nervous," he finished.

"Leave the handling bit to me, but I need to know what is it that *you* want, my darling son?" she asked.

Taking a deep breath, he said, "I am fond of Devika, but not sure if I want to spend the rest of my life with her. Also, I have busted my ass for the past year or so, launching the company and bringing it to where it is today. People may be harbouring the impression that Dad has financed this venture, but you know it was a hundred percent my sheer hard work and negotiation skills which convinced people to invest. And I am very excited about the space I am currently in, professionally. I just want to concentrate on my work right now and nothing else."

"Then why did you not tell her so? Surely she'll understand," argued his mother.

Nodding his head, Aaryan said, "I tried everything, stopping short of being downright rude, but I couldn't shake her off. And then she played the parents card – how happy you guys and her father would be about this!"

Mrs Kapoor wanted to see her son settled, but she would not tolerate anyone arm twisting him.

How dare she try and manipulate my son, fumed Anjali.

Outwardly calm, she said to him, "Don't you worry. Let me try and speak to her. Have faith in your mother and just give me some time. Now go and catch some sleep."

Once Aaryan left, she tried out various permutations and combinations in her head. Finally reaching a conclusion, Mrs Kapoor brought out her phone.

By Friday, Gayatri was thoroughly peeved with Nakul. He was caught up with work and hadn't even tried to come see her since the argument. Depressed, she walked up to Taruna's cubicle to discuss the new appraisal plan that she was working on.

"I'll come later if you are busy," said Gayatri watching Taruna work frantically on her laptop.

Taruna replied, "No no, just wrapping up a few things before heading out. In fact, I was going to come to you to invite you for my party tomorrow."

"Oh, is it your birthday?" asked Gayatri.

"No no, just a special day for me; you'll get to know when you come in," said Taruna. "Don't be late and you are welcome to bring a date,"she added with a wink.

Gayatri sighed. "Not sure about the date, but I'll be there positively."

Aaryan was contemplating whether to say yes or no to the invite, when Devika walked into his cabin.

"I have booked us a table at the Souk tomorrow night at Taj. I know how much you love eating there and after that we are going to my friends' place at Bandra! They are throwing me a 'welcome back home' party," finished Devika.

Irritated at her bossy attitude, Aaryan replied sarcastically, "I am sure you'll have a good time, but I am committed to another engagement already."

Devika came around his desk as she sensed his temper spiking.

She nibbled his earlobe and whispered suggestively, "Change of plan. I'll join in wherever that you are going for drinks and dinner; then I shall take you home and be your dessert!"

"It's an office party and I am not sure if I can take someone along," said Aaryan, attempting to wiggle out of the situation.

"You own the bloody company. I am sure if you want, you can take an army of people," she sniffed.

"I just thought it would be a good idea for me to get to know your colleagues. But if you don't want to be seen with me…" she trailed off, looking downcast.

"Alright, tomorrow evening sharp at seven, don't be late," relented a helpless Aaryan.

Saturday morning, Nakul called Gayatri and apologised for

being super busy the past few days and he promised fervently to make it up to her. Not the kind to hold a grudge for too long, Gayatri caved in and told him about the party that evening and asked him if he could join her.

"Why don't I pick you up at about 7.30ish and and we go for the party? I'll stay over for the weekend and you can bash me up as much as you want then. Now tell me what are you going to wear tonight? Can I request you to wear the hot black thing that we bought the other day?" asked Nakul.

A little surprised at his enthusiasm for the party, Gayatri agreed and put down the phone. Later that evening, she piled her hair up in a chignon and added a pair of chandelier earrings, leaving the arms and neck unadorned in the halter dress. These were her favourite earrings. Nakul had gifted them the previous year on her birthday. The five inch stilettos showed off her curves perfectly in the backless number. With a stroke of blush-on and some smoky eye make-up with a nude lip gloss, she was ready.

Chewing her lower lip, she wondered if she was over-dressed for the occasion. Before she could think of changing anything though, the doorbell rang. Nakul whistled wolfishly as she opened the door.

"Let's not go anywhere, we'll party at home only," he said.

To which Gayatri replied, "We'll have to go for a bit. But I promise to not linger on. You better be ready to make it up to me for the entire week."

Nakul said adoringly, "I am worried about tonight."

At her enquiring look, he clarified, "I am sure I'll embarrass myself by not being able to keep my hands off you in the party."

She blushed at his effusive praise and picked up her keys

and her clutch.

"Congratulations!" everyone screamed when Gayatri and Nakul reached the venue.

Overwhelmed by the gesture, she hugged Taruna to express her thanks.

But Taruna shrugged her aside saying, "This was entirely your guy's plan. He is too good to be true. If I were you, I'd hold on to him tight!"

Turning around, Gayatri spotted Nakul still standing next to the door, talking to someone.

Emotionally charged, she ran to hug him, only to bang into something solid... and warm. Rubbing her eyes free from the moisture, she looked up and realised 'it' was a well-muscled chest and belonged to her boss.

"Are you hurt, Gayatri? What's happened?" AK asked her urgently.

Controlling his sudden urge to wrap his arms around her, Aaryan tipped her face up to wipe a tear which was trickling down her cheek. With visible effort, she broke away from his hypnotic gaze and haltingly explained the reason for her 'happy tears'. Relief coursed through him and he moved away from her.

"Are you alright?" quizzed Nakul when she reached him.

Cursing her transparent face and her hot boss, Gayatri said, "I am more than okay... I just wanted to thank you for the fabulous surprise."

She then started introducing him to the people from her office, whom Taruna had invited on Nakul's behest. She also met his colleagues from HMM, who had come especially for free booze and khana, all the way from Andheri, or so they told her.

Taking him to meet her boss, she said, "AK, this is Nakul, the person I intended to crash into earlier."

Aaryan shook hands with Nakul and introduced Devika. Gayatri thanked them both for coming to the party.

To which Devika countered, "Oh! He takes his job as a boss very seriously and though we had an important event scheduled to attend, Aaryan insisted upon coming here first."

"Lucky me! So sorry that you were inconvenienced because of me though," Gayatri glared at AK and walked away.

"Your boss's girl is very sexy," said Nakul lecherously.

Turning around, Gayatri retorted, "If I was 5'7, with long legs and not a single ounce of fat and wore clothes only made by unpronounceable designers, I would also look very sexy."

"You are jealous…haha. What happened to all that gyan – I am unique and hence no comparison with anyone."

Not wanting to face the fact that her adverse reaction to Devika was due to her link with AK rather than a reaction to Nakul's words, Gayatri pulled him towards her and said, "Let's dance."

Nakul extracted his arm out of her grip and told her, "You don't want me to start the b-school level stuff here, right? Go find a better dance partner, while I entertain the guys from my office."

Left all by herself, Gayatri turned around to find AK walking towards her. She launched herself at him.

"I apologise that you were forced to come here. You are more than welcome to leave anytime," she said in a huff.

AK took her arm, propelled her to a corner and asked, "Are

you always so judgemental and short tempered or is today a special day?"

Looking at her belligerent expression, he continued cheerfully, "Do you not know me enough by now to understand that if I don't want to do something, no one can make me do it? So calm down and enjoy your party."

Aaryan thought back to his reaction when Devika had spoken to Gayatri condescendingly. He had been walking up to Gayatri to apologise for Devika's behaviour but his spitfire HR had beaten him to it, going all aggressive on him. Smiling at the thought, he ordered a drink while Devika sulked in a corner.

Half an hour later, Aaryan decided to call it a night and looked for Gayatri. When had she become Gayatri from Ms Vohra in his head? He finally spotted Taruna and walked up to her to bid adieu.

"Please thank Ms Vohra and her err…friend for inviting Devika and me," he started.

"Why don't you say it yourself, AK? They are right there,"she said pointing to the back of the room.

Aaryan started walking towards the pointed direction only to stop dead in his tracks at the sight of HIS HR dancing in the arms of that skinny nerd. With a string of uncharitable thoughts towards Nakul, he took in Gayatri's closed eyes, a smile hovering on her luscious lips. His eyes zeroed in on her glistening skin, making him want to trace those contours. He could vividly recall the feel of her body pressed against his and the intoxicating smell unique to her. Abruptly realising that he had been staring for far too long, he turned around and walked out of the party with Devika trailing behind.

After bidding rounds of farewell and thanks all around,

Nakul and Gayatri went to settle the bill.

"It's already been paid for," said the manager.

"By whom?" But even as Gayatri asked that question, she knew the answer.

"Damn generous of the man," said Nakul, gaily.

"Thank you my love, for the most amazing party," said Gayatri sleepily, resting her head on Nakul's shoulders as they sped back to her flat.

"Err, I need to talk to you," said Nakul a bit seriously.

"Not tonight please! Anything serious, depressing or related to any lecture on my conduct can wait till tomorrow," she wailed.

Gayatri crashed the minute her head hit the pillow, but Nakul stayed awake for the longest time, thinking about the news that he needed to share with her.

The next morning started with a cranky, slightly hung-over Gayatri waking up to a nervous looking Nakul.

"I have been offered the international stint by the company. I am the first one from our batch to be offered this. I, uh, shall have to move to Singapore immediately," said Nakul in a rush.

She stared at him as if he had sprouted two heads suddenly.

"What are you talking about Nakul? Please don't tell me this is one of your pranks," she cried.

It was Nakul's silence which made Gayatri pause.

"Why the hell did you not tell me about this till now?"she shouted.

Taking a deep breath, Nakul said, "I didn't know that I would be offered this relocation and that too this quickly. Trust me, had I known, I would have never asked you to come to Mumbai."

Incensed at his calm and casual demeanour, Gayatri shouted

back, "Why did you not tell me about this possibility when you asked me to look for a job here?"

Though Nakul tried hard to reason with her, she was in no mood to listen to his explanation. She told him that she didn't want to talk anymore on the topic right then and that he should leave.

Nakul thought about insisting to stay, but then chose another tactic.

"I had thought that you would have been ecstatic hearing the news. But never did I imagine that you would make me feel guilty for my accomplishment."And he left.

Gayatri oscillated between disbelief and anger through the entire weekend. Sobbing hard, she simply couldn't believe that Nakul had hidden such a big development from her. To top it, he had accused her of being selfish. Staying home and feeling depressed wasn't going to help her, so she decided to go to work on Monday morning.

Deciding to take a break from clingy girlfriends and the lure of sexy sirens, Aaryan flew away to the US for a prospective deal on Sunday night.

Gayatri threw herself into all possible kinds of pending work upon reaching office to keep herself occupied. And then came the summons from the big boss himself, Sr Kapoor.

Rohit Kapoor oversaw a lot of companies, but his strength lay in identifying the pulse of any workplace and what made the organization tick. Sitting in his son's office during his absence, Rohit realised that the culture at JBCN could use a little nudge beyond the occasional parties held there and decided to call upon the Human Resources of the company.

Sudhir Mishra and Gayatri found themselves outside

Sr Kapoor's office at 1 p.m.

"Are you alright? You look a little low on spirits today," commented Sudhir.

"Too much partying, sir," was the wobbly reply from Gayatri, and before Sudhir could comment any further, they were asked to go in.

"You are not doing a good job with my employees here, Sudhir," said Sr Kapoor.

Used to Rohit Kapoor's style of functioning, Sudhir replied, "And how would you like me to improve upon that, Mr Kapoor?"

"If I have to tell you everything, what am I paying you for? But since the question has been raised, I shall share my thoughts on it. I believe we can do a little more to motivate the employees. This place is so uninspiring and low on energy,"quipped Rohit.

"Fair enough.We will draw up some ideas and present to you by EOD tomorrow," said Sudhir.

"Why don't we brainstorm right now for some ideas? Let's call some project managers for their inputs as well," replied Sr Kapoor.

It was the worst day for her creativity to be called upon, but Gayatri scolded herself mentally and got ready to do what she did best – 'something different.' Gayatri's ideas ranged from masterchef competitions to townhalls to poker nights. By the end of the hour, they had a lot of interesting ideas to work upon.

Rohit Kapoor thanked everyone and asked them to resume work, except for Sudhir.

"The girl is a good choice, Sudhir. I like her attitude and flexibility. Make sure we retain her," he said.

Sudhir smiled, "I had to fight real hard with AK to hire her initially. He was dead set against her."

"And now?"asked Sr Kapoor intrigued.

Sudhir thought for a minute and replied, "For most of the day-to-day functioning, he interacts with Gayatri only. I am brought in only when a new client comes in or in case of a policy related issue. AK depends quite heavily on her now. I guess he finally recognises and respects her skills."

Rohit knew his son very well. He was also not blind to Gayatri's beauty and charm that he had seen in the past hour. He enquired, a touch too casually, "What about their personal equation? Are they always in agreement?"

Missing the gleam in his eyes, Sudhir replied in all seriousness, "Agreement? There are fireworks every time these two have any discussion. On many occasions, I have had to intervene to settle matters. But I believe a healthy argument leads to a better solution."

After discussing a few more matters with him, Rohit asked Sudhir to carry on with his day. Getting Shweta on the intercom, he asked to be connected to his wife.

"Darling, can you drop into Aaryan's office today for a bit," he asked the moment Mrs Kapoor picked up the phone.

Feeling miserable for the past two days now, Nakul had had enough of this no communication bit from Gayatri. He decided to speak with her, no matter what it took and called up her office number. Not wanting to become fodder for the receptionist's gossip, Gayatri reluctantly took his call.

"What do you want? Am busy right now," said Gayatri angrily.

"You must be busy preparing for your Singapore posting," she ranted.

"Just give me a chance to explain this properly, please. Abuse me, throttle me, but don't give me this silent treatment babe," pleaded Nakul.

She thought back to their argument which had left her feeling unsure about her own self. Was she being selfish in feeling betrayed by him? Was she overreacting?

Her anger stemmed from the fact that while he had dictated her long term career path, he hadn't bothered even 'informing' her about his plans till the last minute. Gayatri still couldn't believe that Nakul was moving to Singapore by the end of the month for at least a couple of years.

"What is there to explain, Nakul? I understood perfectly well what you told me that day," she said.

"Can we please meet and talk?" he asked.

She eventually relented and agreed to meet him for dinner.

Nakul drank in the sight of Gayatri as she sat down in front of him later that evening. She looked resplendent in a red sleeveless crop top and denims with her hair braided. For him, she stood out in the crowd like a colourful exotic butterfly, his butterfly.

"We both have an early start tomorrow, so let's get started, shall we?" said Gayatri.

Nakul chose his words carefully, "For the past few months, there has been a buzz about a foreign posting, but that was to come through after a year or so. It was only by the time you reached Mumbai that I started getting an inkling that the relocation may come my way sooner than later. But I also thought that JBCN seemed like a good opportunity for you and by the time I would relocate, you would have settled in here. And then as soon as I found my feet at the Singapore office, we would figure out our future plans. Please believe me when I say this, you are more important to me than anything else and if you tell me, I won't take up this posting."

She smiled sadly, "Do you realise that in the entire speech you just gave, it was all about you and what you thought and what you deemed right. I and my thoughts didn't feature anywhere. You know me well enough to predict that I would never ever ask you to stay back. So please spare me the theatrics. I thought we have always shared everything with each other. But all that doesn't matter anymore. The one thing that rankles me… is your complete disregard for my career. What exactly do you expect me to do now – follow you to Singapore or wait for you to come back?'

Without giving him a chance to respond, she forged ahead, "I like my job here and am going to stick to it. I feel as of now, we should both give precedence to our respective careers and see where that takes us."

"Are you trying to break up with me?" he choked out.

Calmly, she replied, "No, I am not. I am just giving you the freedom to go pursue your dreams. I thought you would have been happy about my not throwing a tantrum."

Nakul was nonpulsed at Gayatri's attitude. For the first time, he didn't know whether to push her further or wait for her anger to subside. For the past few days, he had been blaming himself for holding back on the information. In all honesty, he had never imagined Gayatri would react so strongly. Nakul tried to reassure himself that she would come around with time and started to tell her about his plans.

"I'll have to go home for a couple of days before I fly out. Dad's retirement has been postponed and he has been offered an advisory role in his firm. So Didi and I have decided to fly down from Delhi and Mumbai respectively, to spend some time with them," he started.

Born in a lower middle class family, Nakul was the younger of the two children. A bright and sincere student, he had a lifelong burning desire to uplift his family's financial and social status to dizzying heights. With his sister married and well settled in Delhi, Nakul now wanted to quickly earn enough, enabling his parents a secure and comfortable retired life. He had introduced Gayatri to his mother during their B-School days and had shared his true feelings.

Unfortunately, his mother's initial reaction hadn't been heartening, "Isn't she too pretty? Mostly such girls are vain and self-centred."

He had countered it by listing Gayatri's virtues.

"Maa, she is extremely down to earth. bright, yet modest and she is very loving. Her best quality is to be able to see beneath a person's surface and value his qualities. Please don't make any assumptions about her till you know her better," he had finished passionately.

"I hope it's true for your sake, my son," she had replied, not sounding very convinced.

Not very highly educated herself, Mrs Shrivastava valued hard work and simplicity uppermost in a girl, together with a subservient attitude towards her man, and this girl seemed to fit none of those categories.

Coming back to the present, he thought that had they not fought over his relocation, he could have persuaded her to come along to spend some time with his parents.

"Maybe on the next visit to India, I'll do so," he told himself.

"My friend Rachna is working in Singapore. She can help you with shifting and settling down. I will mail her tonight and pass on her contact details to you," said Gayatri, as a sign of peace-offering.

"Isn't she the one who studied with you at school?" asked Nakul.

"Yup, you will like her. She is pragmatic and extremely career focussed, just like you," she finished a touch sarcastically.

Nakul immediately said, "There is only one girl that I like, rather, am crazy about. She is the centre of my universe."

"I meant like her as a person, nothing more. There is no need to wax poetry in my honour," she said drily.

Not waiting for his reaction, Gayatri quietly concentrated on her chicken skewers. She just wished for the dinner to get over quickly. Her heart was breaking and she didn't know what to do about it.

A decently pretty girl usually has her share of admirers while growing up and so did Gayatri, but her heart had never been engaged before meeting Nakul. Even after the first six months of their relationship, she had been unsure about her feelings for him. But eventually, she had decided to jump into the deep end and it had been absolutely wonderful, up until now!

Gayatri declined Nakul's offer to drop her home.

"I am now fairly familiar with the way Mumbai works and

would be doing things alone here in the near future. So why not start from tonight itself?" she asked.

Avoiding a potential landmine, Nakul agreed to let her go after extracting a promise to spend the entire weekend together before he left for Singapore.

Next day at work, Gayatri asked Sudhir for leave for a few days in the coming week for Diwali since she wanted to spend it with her parents.

"With all the new projects that Sr Kapoor wants to start, I am not sure if I'll be able to spare you till the end of the month," he replied apologetically.

She had no choice but to immerse herself totally into work, pulling in long working hours.

By the end of the fortnight, they had started two more HR initiatives, leaving her barely any time to eat and sleep. But she was enjoying the commotion and the tremendous response from the employees. With Nakul visiting his parents, Gayatri spent the weekends in office too, leaving her no time to mull over her personal issues.

On his way back from the airport, Aaryan thought about his successful trip where he had managed to clinch the deal with a new big client. It was a big feather in JBCN's cap!

"Take me to the office first," he instructed the driver.

Saturday evening was mostly deserted at JBCN so he wasn't ready for the sight of his, even lovelier than before HR, dressed in faded, figure hugging denims with a Superman tee and hair tied in a bun. She looked like a ripe strawberry, good enough to eat.

Embarrassed at being caught in ratty clothes at office,

Gayatri acknowledged AK, who seemed to have stepped right out of a GQ billboard.

"Do you have nowhere better to be on a Saturday evening?" he asked.

"I had some pending work. I am just leaving now. Have a good weekend," she said and tried to move away.

Without thinking, Aaryan took hold of her arm and turned her back to face him, "Would you like to grab a quick bite before you head home, unless you have other plans?"

Taken aback at the unexpected invite, Gayatri hesitated before answering, "Thanks AK, but I am very tired today. Appreciate the offer though!"

"I totally understand, another time," he said, releasing her arm and stepping aside.

Aaryan pondered over the reactions Gayatri brought out in him. There was a weird possessiveness that he felt towards her. Thinking back to his impromptu invite, Aaryan realised that she hadn't been her usual chirpy self and he had felt the urge to make her blues go away.

"I need to stay away from her or I shall end up making a fool of myself. Have enough shit piled up on my plate as is, with Devika stalking my every move. I need to ask Mom whether she managed to figure out a solution to this fast deteriorating situation," he grimaced.

It had been tough refusing AK. Gayatri had been sorely tempted, partly because there was a strange pull that she always felt towards him, and partly due to her feelings towards Nakul these days. It was mainly due to the latter though that she ended up refusing his offer. It wouldn't have been fair to either one of them had she decided to go out with AK, just to spite Nakul!

Nakul was enjoying his stay with his family. The issues with Gayatri were also almost sorted. Maybe she was still a little upset about the whole thing, but he was sure that she would come around eventually. He was eagerly looking forward to the new phase in his life, starting next week.

"I'll plan a visit for her to Singapore, once I am settled in, as a surprise. She would love it, I am sure," he grinned to himself.

On his flight back to Mumbai from Indore, Nakul realised that Rachna had been a great help the past few days and he had Gayatri to thank for connecting him with her. Not only had she found him decent accommodation, but also finalised the paperwork on his behalf. She had also assured him that she would arrange an Indian cook for him, which took the load completely off his shoulders.

The next few days flew past very quickly for him. Before he realised, it was time for him to board the flight. Gayatri had come to see him off at the airport and he tried desperately to find the warmth in her eyes. In the last two days, she had seemed polite and aloof. But as a master strategist, he realised this wasn't the time to raise that point, so he simply hugged her and shared one last kiss before going into the terminal.

Gayatri was left behind with a sense of bewilderment in a city full of strangers. She missed him and was lonely, but her heart didn't seem to be bleeding.

▼

On the other hand, time flew for Nakul as he landed and settled into a routine quickly. The work environment was challenging and exciting and so was the city.

"Hi Rachna, so we finally meet face-to-face,' he said as the dusky beauty stood in front of him.

At five feet three inches, she was a miniature version of Bipasha Basu, or so he thought. With a cute dimple and curly hair, she was a vision in her smart office wear.

Reaching up to hug him, she said, "I feel like I already know you, having heard so much from Gayatri. How is she, by the way? I haven't been able to catch up with her this last week."

Assuring her that Gayatri was doing fine, Nakul asked, "Were you particularly close friends since school?"

"Not bum-chums, but I would say we have managed to stay friendly all these years," she said and got down to ordering food.

After the initial hectic days at HMM's office, he had finally managed to plan this dinner with Rachna.

"So, have you done any sightseeing till now, or just been cooped up at work?"she asked.

He had to admit that he had been too caught up with work and settling into his new accommodation, and hadn't ventured out beyond the local supermarket around his flat.

"We must rectify that asap!" she exclaimed.

She continued, "I am a workaholic myself, but come Saturday, I need to get my Jimmy Choos out. You know what I mean?"

Nodding his head, he let her take the lead and plan the next evening out for him.

With no friends or acquaintances in town, he was happy to tag along with her, wherever she chose to go. Rachna introduced him to most of her friends and ensured he was having a good time in the city. After a month or so of meeting up every weekend, they were sitting at a lounge in Ministry of Sound. She had more or less gauged his personality by now and genuinely liked him. That evening she challenged him to an impromptu drinking match. Thinking of Gayatri, who was a teetotaller and got knocked off after just one glass of wine, Nakul assumed she was in a similar category and agreed to the challenge.

"The first one to throw up would be the loser and the winner gets to decide his/her prize. Are you ready, Mr Shrivastava?" she said.

Puffing up his chest, he replied, "Bring it on!"

By the fifth shot, he was barely managing to stand up while she looked extremely normal, almost sober. Only her high pitched laughter gave her away.

"I think you should stop now," he said, his words slurring slightly.

Laughing, she punched him lightly in the chest, "Says the man who doesn't know whether he is standing or sitting."

By the eighth shot, he was fully sloshed. A not so steady Rachna dragged him to his feet and called for a cab. She fished for his keys as they reached his flat and managed to open the door, with him almost draped on her shoulders. She pushed him onto the sofa in his living room. She got a comforter from the bedroom and pulled it over a now comatose Nakul. She brushed his hair tenderly away from his eyes and then couldn't help herself and kissed him gently on his forehead and lips. She went to his room, deciding to stay the night.

In his bed, engulfed in his smell, Rachna realised that she was halfway in love with him. She thought of all the wonderful times they had spent together recently. His sense of humour and easy going nature had slowly converted the liking to much stronger emotions without her realising it. Her eyes fell on the photo frame kept next to the bed, displaying Gayatri and Nakul laughing and hugging each other. Suddenly deflated, she put a lid on her thoughts and tried to sleep.

▼

Gayatri was terribly lonely and homesick. Work was the only steady anchor in her life and she had started going to office on weekends regularly now. All the hard work had started to show results and she was getting meatier assignments. They had also decided to hire an assistant manager to aid her. This was a fantastic achievement for her within the first six months of her tenure.

Sudhir dropped by at her cubicle on Thursday to invite her for a dinner at his place the following evening.

"It's my wedding anniversary and we have called a few friends over," he informed her.

"Sure, thanks for inviting me. I shall be there," she replied.

He said, "Great! See you sharp at eight. Darla has directions to my home."

Deciding to wear Indian for the dinner, Gayatri brought out her favourite green sequined saree with a matching chiffon tube blouse, knotted at the back. In a mood to cheer herself up, she glammed up a bit by applying eye shadow and mascara, finishing with kajal in her eyes. Going with glossed nude lips, she completed her toilette with a few sprays of her favourite perfume and picked up the gift wrapped pair of pearl frames for her hosts.

She met Rohit Kapoor and his lovely wife as she got off

the taxi outside Sudhir's residence on Marine Drive. During previous few encounters, the lady had been extremely gracious and warm towards Gayatri.

At the same time, Anjali was recalling her conversation with Rohit about how their son had shown an interest in Gayatri.

"I can't remember the last time Aaryan fought with any girl, professionally or otherwise. He is either indifferent or extremely charming to them," he had said on the phone to Anjali.

Since then, Anjali had dropped into the office a few times and had managed to get a glimpse of the chemistry between her son and Gayatri. Much to her delight, the two of them reminded her of a younger version of Rohit and herself.

Hugging her warmly, Anjali gave Gayatri a once over and beamed, "You are going to knock their socks off! I love a woman who can carry her saree well. It shows her ability to handle the most intricate complications which life may throw at her."

Though Anjali Kapoor had solved the mystery of Devika a long time ago, she had decided to hold off its resolution with the introduction of Gayatri into the picture. Knowing her son, he would have bolted at the first hint of any matchmaking on his mother's part and this dinner was going to provide a good opportunity to see their interaction up, close and personal. With Gayatri looking the way she was, Anjali Kapoor had no doubts about her son's reaction.

Gayatri wished the couple and walked towards her colleagues. Without losing a beat, Anjali drew Sudhir's wife, Kamna towards the kitchen. Good friends since their adolescence days, Kamna knew that her old friend was up to some mischief.

'How do you like the girl, Gayatri?' asked Mrs Kapoor.

"She is too old for my teenage sons and too young for my husband,"came the pat reply.

Not to be detracted by her friend's bad sense of humour, Anjali forged ahead, "I think they'll make a great pair together."

Kamna replied, "I have a feeling that she may prove to be a bit too much for your son."

Sudhir walked into the ladies' whispered conversation and said, "At least wait for the party to start properly before you indulge in your gossiping."

Anjali countered immediately, "Wait till your son turns thirty and is still single and see if you don't come to me for help."

Shushing them both, Kamna told them to fight it out later. "We have a party to host, so if you both can do your respective duties right now, I'll be highly obliged."

Saying so, she propelled them outside the kitchen door.

Devika had latched onto AK like a leech ever since he had come back from the US. He had thought about strangling her a couple of times since the time they had walked into the party. He moved away in relief as Devika answered a call and he saw 'his HR'. Looking jaw dropping gorgeous, his hungry gaze took in the hair tied in a loose bun, with big gold loops hanging in the ears, to the alluringly exposed creamy shoulders to the almost poetic curve at the waist, finishing at her patent red toe nails peeping out of the strappy gold heels.

"What the hell is she thinking? Wearing such clothes in public," he muttered to himself.

His mother was just in time to catch his reaction.

She said, "You look upset. Is something the matter?"

He spluttered, "Something is definitely the matter. That girl, that woman… she has no sense of dressing up in an official party. Can you see that thing draped around her? It's threatening to fall off any minute now? Can you see how much skin is being exposed?"

Elated at his reaction, Anjali Kapoor turned to look at Gayatri and said, "I can't see anything wrong with her saree. I would rather say that she is wearing more yards of cloth than at least three of the women present here, put together, including your dear Devika."

She continued, "I personally think she is looking lovely and checking the expressions on the faces of the men around her, I feel they agree."

Too busy staring at her, he had failed to see all the male attention being bestowed upon Gayatri, which incensed him further.

"Kamna is calling me. I'll be back." Her mission accomplished, she moved away from her already distracted son.

"Should we leave now? It'll take us forty-five minutes to reach the airport even at this hour. My father should be landing by then," asked Devika?

Thinking quickly about how to get out of his commitment given to her earlier, he replied, "Umm… there is a slight problem. Dad wants me to stick around here a little longer. An important client is going to join us afterwards. So why don't you carry on and go pick up your father? I'll come around and see him tomorrow, I promise."

Petulant at the sudden change in plan, Devika thought about throwing a fit, but refrained due to his parents' presence. The minute she left the party, Aaryan walked up to the side bar and requested for a single malt. Drowning it in a gulp, he felt almost ready to face his nearly naked girl (yes, she was almost naked… no matter what logic his mother gave!).

"Hi guys!" he said walking up to the group where Gayatri stood with the others.

Dhruv immediately quipped, "Point to be noted – only after his hot girl left the party, has AK decided to bless us with his presence."

With everyone laughing, he used the opportunity to draw Gayatri aside and said, "I want you to work on the new project that we are going to take up, in the role of a project manager. We will need your skills for this one."

Pleasantly surprised, she could only nod in response.

"We'll talk about this in detail Monday morning," he finished.

Gayatri could see the sexy stubble shadowing his jaw and felt a quickening of her pulse in such close proximity to him.

He reached out to hold her arm and said, "Have you seen the view from Sudhir's house?"

Without waiting for an answer, he pulled her towards the French windows opening into the balcony. They stood in darkness which was dispelled only by the full moon. Gayatri's senses were being assaulted by the whiff of AK's perfume and his nearness. His hand still on her arm, Aaryan struggled to come up with a topic to prolong the moment.

"Your girlfriend left early?"quizzed Gayatri breaking the silence.

He replied, "She has gone to receive her father from the airport," in a tone signalling end of discussion on that topic.

Striving for a change, he asked, "So am I ever going to be

treated to the now famous rajma chawal of yours? Also, dad has been singing your praises with all the new initiatives in the company. The energy levels are visibly higher amongst the staff."

A dazzling smile lit up her entire face at the compliment and Aaryan wished they were anywhere but here, amongst his family and employees.

She didn't want him to see how much his sheer presence was affecting her being. Before she ended up doing something foolish, she decided to walk away.

"I think I'll go and ask if I can be of any help to Mrs Mishra," she told him.

Wordlessly, Aaryan moved aside, allowing her to pass. He remained outside for a few moments to calm his rush of blood. No longer fighting his attraction for her, Aaryan decided to take it as it came.

The dining table had been set with a buffet spread rivalling that of a five-star hotel and the menu varied from Indian to Thai to Italian. Piling her plate, Gayatri walked towards her friends who were already stuffing their faces. AK joined them and managed to stand right next to her, their bodies almost touching.

"If you are done with your food, should we go have a look at the dessert options,"said the wretched man as if he could read her conflicted thoughts.

Taruna immediately chipped in, "Did you know that Gayatri has a weakness for hazelnut cake with mascarpone. She calls it orgasmic."

Giving a death stare to her friend, Gayatri wished that the ground would split open and she could plunge right into it. Not daring to meet anyone's eyes, she walked towards the kitchen to hand over her plate to the staff. Turning, she almost bumped into AK, who had crept up behind her.

"Don't say a word. I'll kill that girl with my bare hands," she said through clenched teeth.

Finding her embarrassment endearing, he said, "Oh c'mon, it's not so bad. I'll tell you what, let's chuck the... err... orgasmic dessert. Lemme treat you to a nice paan. Have you tried it at Volga yet?"

She shook her head, "No I haven't and frankly I don't mind. But how far is this place and will I get a taxi back?"

He congratulated himself silently, "Not too far and don't worry about transport. Let's go say our thanks to the hosts."

As they bid good-byes to Mrs and Mr Mishra, Anjali winked at her husband at her apparent success.

Giving her a hug, Sr Kapoor smilingly said, "There is absolutely no match to you, my love!"

Gayatri looked at the two-seater low slung car and thought, "It's going to be a challenge getting inside this beauty in the saree."

What she didn't realise was the close proximity that the car would offer once both were seated. Cocooned together, Gaytri felt AK's hand brush her thigh (accidentally or so she assumed) as he switched gears.

"This was a very bad idea," she told herself.

Covertly, Aaryan studied Gayatri's profile as she sat deep in thought. He wondered if she could hear the loud banging of his heart beat against its walls; he hadn't been this nervous or excited since grade eight, on his first real date with the very sexy Dia! Throttling the engine, they took off towards Fort, swivelling through nearly empty lanes.

Upon reaching there, he asked Gayatri if she wanted to step

out of the car and wait for their paans.

With a self-depreciating laugh, she replied, "I am not sure how I managed to get inside the car with the whole ensemble intact. Don't think I'll be able to repeat the feat anytime soon."

"Let me help you with it," he said hastily.

He opened the door and held out both his hands. She hesitated a little before swinging out her legs. She placed her fingers in AK's outstretched hands, pulling herself out of the car. He released her hands and placed his palm at the small of her back guiding her towards the rear end of the car. He came and stood next to her, their bodies almost touching. She felt a sizzle go through her from head to toe. She moved away a bit as the man returned with their order.

"I haven't had a paan in ages!" she exclaimed.

To which he replied drily, "You mean ever since you moved to Mumbai."

A surprised Gayatri asked, "How did you guess?"

"I am getting used to your habit of extrapolating things a bit," he said ironically.

She retorted, "You mean I exaggerate? Saying that I haven't eaten a paan in six months wouldn't sound as much fun as ages, right? It's just to make the conversation a bit livelier, though *that* would be an alien concept to you, no?"

"You mean I am not a good conversationalist?" he asked softly.

"Or, are you by any chance suggesting that my company is boring, hmm…? We would have to rectify that impression asap," he said silkily.

He turned to face her and closed the distance between them,

taking the paan from her fingers. Before she could question what he was doing, Aaryan swooped down to plant an open-mouthed kiss on her lips.

"I had wanted to do that the entire bloody evening," he muttered to himself.

Shaking her befuddled head, Gayatri spluttered, "Wh-what in the hell did you do that for?"

"I was wondering how you taste and now I know. Just a peck to make things livelier," he shrugged.

Almost hysterical, she shouted, "Peck? You call this a peck? Are you mad?"

Before she could draw another breath, he bent his head down again and effectively silenced her. He ran his fingers through her luxurious hair, dropping the pins down from them. He received no resistance from her except a muted whimper. He discovered that saree was now his favourite clothing for women.

Only the repeatedly discreet coughing from nearby quarters brought him back to his senses. Some middle-aged people standing a few feet away from Aaryan's car had looks ranging from amusement to mild disapproval.

One of the women commented sympathetically, "I am sure they are newly married, living in a joint family," while others hooted.

Horrified at being the centre of such speculation, she tugged at the sleeve of a bemused AK and whispered urgently, "Let's go from here."

Nodding, he deposited Gayatri on her seat and started the car.

She tried explaining the directions to her flat, but AK looked at her and simply said, "I know where you live."

Mortified at her wanton behaviour, Gayatri didn't make any conversation (not that she was capable of it at the moment) and they reached her place in no time.

Forestalling her as she tried to open the car door, he said, "It has been brewing between us for some time now and was bound to happen, if not today, then tomorrow. There are two ways that we can handle this: either behave all uptight and awkward every time we meet each other or accept that this kiss happened and simply move on."

"I am *not* in the habit of kissing every single person I meet, so forgive me if I am having trouble digesting all of this and *simply* moving on. And no, I am not blaming you entirely for this. I w-was an equal participant, but now this is decidedly awkward, whether you admit it or not. Considering you were with your girlfriend, who as per the rumour, is nearly your fiancée, a couple of hours ago, *your* whole behaviour is condemnable," she finished in a huff.

Devika's mention added to the throbbing frustration of being so near, yet so far from her.

He growled back her, "If it was so morally distasteful to you, then all you had to say was *no*. But what I heard were some encouraging sounds. I got carried away. Let's leave it at that, shall we? And all I meant by my earlier statement was that you are critical to the company and I don't want any momentary distraction between us to affect your performance or our work equation."

Feeling flattered and deflated at the same time, Gayatri simply nodded her head and got out of the car.

▼

Disoriented, Nakul got up from the extremely uncomfortable sofa with his head all fuzzy. Following his nose to the aroma of freshly brewed coffee, he discovered a daisy fresh Rachna standing in his kitchenette in his tee and shorts.

"I am terribly sorry for last night's miserable performance," he muttered sheepishly.

Looking at his embarrassed face, she decided to tease him a little and said, "Considering you fell asleep in the middle of kissing me, I don't think I can forgive you so easily."

He felt the ground slip from under his feet as he tried frantically to recall the previous night's events and came up with a blank.

He looked at her pleadingly and she burst out laughing, "Just look at you face right now. Priceless! You look positively horrified."

Only half jokingly, she continued, "Am I that repulsive?"

Hastening to reassure her, Nakul replied, "No no, of course not. It's just that I can't even dream about any friend of Gayatri's in such a manner."

Unaware that he had said absolutely the last thing that she wanted to hear, he continued, "You scared the daylights out of me just now. But thank you so very much. It's obvious that you brought me back to the apartment all by yourself. I am somewhat a lightweight when it comes to drinking. Forgive me."

Wishing that she had never touched the topic, she replied, "Of course, don't worry and it wasn't too much trouble in the end. Anyway, I should be also getting back now. I'll see you around."

Taking her by the arm, he stopped her and said, "This is not done. Please allow me to make up for last night. Let's go grab a nice lunch somewhere and then I shall escort you to your place, as I should have done yesterday."

Protesting, she started, "But I have no clothes to wear. This tee and shorts are yours and…"

"And have never looked any better. Just gimme twenty minutes," he finished for her.

With the coffee mug in his hand, Nakul went to get ready as she tidied up the kitchen, lost in her thoughts, "He is too much in love with her to even think about anyone else. Do I really want to do this to myself *again*? Choosing the wrong guy?"

Rachna Duggal, born to her parents as the second girl out of the three daughters, had found herself madly in love with the college hunk for the first time in her life. Her love was not only reciprocated, but was elevated to an obsession. Her senior by two years, Gautam showered all kinds of attention on her, so much so that she had no time left for anyone else. But the relationship turned poisonous and nasty within months, leaving her wary of all men, until Nakul.

I don't feel threatened or suffocated by him. He genuinely listens to what I have to say, but doesn't mollycoddle me, she thought coming back to the present while standing in Nakul's living room.

Maybe life is giving me a second chance at love, with him. And if Gayatri wants to keep him, she *will* get a fair fight from me. I am sure he shall be appreciated and loved more by me than her. After this pep talk to herself, Rachna decided to actively but subtly woo him.

"Hey," she called out, "what if we were to change the plan? How does a simple Indian home cooked meal sound to you instead?"

Coming out of his room, Nakul grinned and said, "It sounds wonderful, but neither do I have any of the requisite ingredients at home, nor any culinary skills to offer any help to you."

She reached up and ruffled his hair before replying, "I am fully aware of the facts, Mr Shrivastava. What I meant though, was that we go to my place where I get to freshen up, wear my own clothes and dish up some absolutely desi khana while you simply laze around there."

Nakul gravely reverted, "Put like that, no man in his senses shall *ever* refuse your offer."

▼

It had been a week since the dinner at the Mishras', but Gayatri simply couldn't get that night's events out of her mind. Making out like teenagers in full public view was something Gayatri had never done, even at the age when her hormones had raced ahead of her senses! Appalled did not begin to describe what she felt every time she thought about it. To make it worse, it had been him who had finally broken off that mind numbing kiss. Had it been left to her, god only knows what would have happened.

Her chemistry with Nakul had always been great, full of masti and teasing and emotions. But *this* was something else. The sizzling, almost burning desire to be consumed by AK was driving her nuts.

"For the first time, I have been bitten by lust, it seems," she admitted reluctantly to herself, refusing to name it anything deeper than that.

"But I can't let it continue like this. I love working at JBCN and I am not going to let my suddenly awake, horny hormones jeopardise that. AK was right in what he said that night," Gayatri gave herself a stern talk.

She was anxious about working in close proximity with AK henceforth. As a project manager, she had already had a few meetings where he had described her role and responsibilities. The hilarious part was that he seemed to be absolutely normal, bordering on platonically friendly behaviour during these interactions. On the other hand, she had stood in his office tensed and ready to burst into flames at the slightest provocation!

God's cruelty knew no bounds. Not only had he given the guy looks but also an easy charm which could turn fairly intelligent women into tongue-tied ninnies.

Gayatri brought herself back to the present as she waited for her new assistant manager, Radhika to join work. All the project team members except her were working out of New York at the client's site while she and AK coordinated with them out of the Mumbai office. The project itself was slated to take off two weeks later.

Why don't I go home the next weekend? Maybe by not breathing the same air as *him*, I'll be cured of this 'L' ailment of mine. She shot off a leave request to Sudhir.

Aaryan waited impatiently for the time of his scheduled meeting with Gayatri. For the past few days, these encounters had been the highlight of his days. He was finding it increasingly difficult to act normally around her and feared that his affection towards her would become transparent anytime. The only reason stopping him from revealing his feelings to his beautiful HR was to make her like him first!

As for the other man in her life, considering she was at office nearly seven days of the week, he didn't think there was much happening at that end. He wanted her to get to know him and to have her open up to him as well. Other issues could be handled as and when the time came!

But what this spelt for him were two things – first, get rid of the leech named Devika, with or without his mother's help, and second, find out as much as possible about Gayatri, starting with her employment file in his hands.

Realising that it was Gayari's birthday the coming Saturday, he thought hard about what could be done without it looking like a big deal, but still end up being special for her. He finally came up with the plan to hold a special screening of the upcoming rom-com movie on Friday for his entire staff and after, they could ring in her birthday by cutting a cake at the coffee place next door.

Aaryan decided to not rush things and to keep it a low-key corporate affair, just another employee's birthday which happened to coincide with everyone coming together for a night out.

Grinning to himself, he spoke aloud, "I promise to make our next special occasion spectacular."

He descended down to the fourth floor, to reach Gayatri's cubicle.

"Hi, got a minute?" he asked.

Taken aback at his first and unannounced visit to her cabin, she scrambled to get out of her chair.

"O-ofcourse AK. Sorry for all the clutter around. Actually Radhika and I haven't had the time to allocate files and space between ourselves till now," she babbled.

Enjoying her flustered demeanour, he waited patiently while she removed some files and coffee mugs from a chair. Then she sat down with her legs tucked primly under the chair.

"I had just come down to inform you of the movie plan for Friday. We are holding a special showing of that night's new release for the entire staff. Show is at 10 p.m. and it is your job to coordinate with the various teams across the board. Please see to it that we have maximum attendance," he finished.

Frowning at the sudden glitch in her plans, she began tentatively, "Of course AK. But there is a slight issue. I will coordinate the whole event, but won't be present on that night for the screening."

His eyebrows clashed, "What do you mean? Why won't you be there? It is especially important that the HR presence is visible in all corporate events."

She said, "Well, it is my birthday the next day and my parents wanted me to fly down for it. I have already taken the necessary approval from Sudhir. My flight is on Friday afternoon and I'll be back in office by Monday."

He recovered from the unexpected curve ball thrown his way, "Of course you must go. I wasn't aware of your plan. Sudhir and Radhika shall do the needful. You have a great trip!"

With that, he walked out of her cabin, rueing his bad timing and wondering how he could salvage the situation.

Born to a pair of highly successful and accomplished parents, Aaryan had always had to try harder at everything, be it sports, academics or socialising, to come out of their shadow and match up to people's expectations from the Kapoor son. And it had only made him more determined, more focussed with a never-say-die attitude. So if he wanted to be with Gayatri on her birthday, he would find a way, somehow or the other.

Walking with this thought in his head, he entered the 'private' lift earmarked for him… too late! The vice-like grip of Devika held his neck as she attempted to kiss him, suck the life out of him rather.

"What are you doing here?" he asked, trying to wriggle out of her grasp.

"You have been avoiding me, making some excuse or the other. Didn't even come to meet Dad that day as promised. What is going on with you?" she demanded.

Thinking about a particular hazel eyed beauty occupying his mind 24 x 7 these days, he scrambled to come up with a plausible reason to ward her off as they reached his office. He shut his office door in the face of his 'curious' assistant Shweta. He made Devika sit down on one of the plush sofas.

He took a deep breath and started, "Babe, this is not working out between us. I am always caught up at work and I don't think it's fair on you. To be honest, I did warn you about it in the beginning itself. I hate to keep cancelling our plans again and again. But the truth is, I am totally married to my work and it is likely to stay this way for the next few years. Why should you waste your time on a relationship which has nothing to give you? As your true friend, I would advise you to move on and find someone who would give you all the affection and attention that you deserve."

Aaryan lauded himself silently on an Oscar worthy performance, but he didn't think it would have been enough to satisfy her. Hence he was extremely surprised, not to mention suspicious when she meekly agreed with him and did not argue back. She simply walked out of his office.

Devika seethed with the realisation that Kapoor Jr was trying to wiggle out of his commitment. This she simply couldn't allow.

He thinks that I can't see through his juvenile act, she fumed.

Her well-laid future plans depended upon snaring him and becoming Mrs Devika Aaryan Kapoor. Only then her status and reputation would be restored!

I know exactly how to bring him to his knees. Like all boys, his Achilles' heel is his mother and that's who will help me now! she thought on her way to the Kapoor residence at Malabar Hill.

Having called ahead, she was greeted by Anjali herself at the main lobby of the house.

She waited patiently as Devika poured out her grief to her, with sobs and sniffs punctuating her performance. When she reached the part about Aaryan being commitment phobic, Anjali realised that time had come to end this charade.

"My dear, why don't you settle down. Can I get you some chamomile tea or some fresh mogra water?" she asked solicitously.

"You know you are like a daughter to me and I would indeed be very happy if this match was to happen. But I have absolutely no influence over my son's wishes. If he has decided something, then there is really nothing that I can do about it," she started.

She raised a hand to silence Devika's protest and continued in a pleasant voice, "Also, I think in the light of the recent occurrences in your life, it would be in your best interest to take a break from any *new* alliances."

The colour drained out from Devika's face but she brazenly said, "I am not sure what events you are referring to, aunty."

Tut-tutting, Anjali said, "Having been caught in bed with your best friend's fiancé a night before their wedding was bad enough. But it could have been salvaged, had the groom gone ahead and married you. Apparently you had claimed that's what he had promised you. But rumour has it, not only did he call you a one night mistake but also asserted that you came onto him while he was inebriated. What a sorry affair it has been and I am sure you also need some time to come to terms with the loss of face and the humiliation that you must have gone through."

Check-mated, Devika had no come back. She didn't even attempt defending herself any longer. Murmuring an incoherent sentence, Devika hurried out of the house.

"It's Gayatri's birthday tomorrow," an excited Nakul told Rachna over the phone. "I am flying out to Delhi tonight, to spend the weekend with her. It's a surprise for her. Her mother and I planned it out last week," he finished excitedly.

Rachna was flummoxed, to put it mildly.

"B-but you never told me about it last week or even this Wednesday when we met for lunch," she shot at him.

Taken aback slightly at her militant tone, he said, "Leave approval came through last evening, so I didn't get a chance."

She felt as if someone had punched her in the stomach. The past couple of weeks had been wonderful and she thought they were really connecting.

"Anything that I do is useless. He can't see anything beyond her. What the hell do I do to make him notice me, and more importantly, want me?" she thought furiously.

Happy to be back home that Friday evening, Gayatri spent a couple of cosy hours with her mother catching up on all the gossip and sharing her own, of course the censored version!

"I was missing the winters so badly there. The concept of cold hands and warm sweaters doesn't exist in that city," she lamented enjoying Delhi's January cold.

"I want to talk to you about something, Mom," she started seriously after dinner.

Concerned at her tone, Mrs Vohra asked, "What is it, Gattu?"

Gayatri stood up from the bed and started pacing, "I have been conflicted about my feelings for Nakul these past months. First I thought that I was upset about the way he had taken me for granted. I had wondered if he thought that I was such a shallow person that I could be *handled* with surprise parties and gifts. But that is not what the problem is now."

Registering her mother's surprised look, she continued, "I am feeling disconnected from him. There is no ache or longing inside me every time I think of him. The conversations feel stilted or worse, superficial. It's like I have fallen out of love. I feel like a terrible person. What is wrong with me, Maa?"

Neena wanted to tell her daughter that she had seen this coming long ago; that everything Gayatri had felt for Nakul had been admiration turned into fondness. She was tempted to explain the difference between the 'happy mild affection' and the 'all consuming burning messy love'.

But she simply hugged her daughter and said, "Some matters need to be left to our hearts. What I mean by that filmy line is – let your emotions flow naturally. Don't analyse. Go by your instinct; but you definitely need to tell the other person how you feel."

Gayatri felt guilty that she hadn't told her mother about her emotions for Aaryan. But she still didn't know how she felt about him. So she went to bed brooding.

Worried about Nakul's surprise visit the next morning, there was nothing that Mrs Vohra could do about it at this moment.

Pleased with himself at the last minute manoeuvres, Aaryan went over the plan in his head as his private jet was about to touch down at the Delhi airport. In order for him to draw her out of her home, especially on her birthday, required an urgent and valid reason. He had hit upon the idea of attending a conference being held in Delhi. Aryan's new client was coincidentally flying down for it. This seemed to be the perfect excuse.

Nakul's flight landed at 7 a.m. and he went straight to his friends' flat for a quick cup of tea. Soon after, he sat in the cab and took out the gift envelope meant for the birthday girl. Nakul's spirits were quite buoyed by the thought of surprising his girl. He reached Gayatri's residence and rang the bell.

With dreams about sexy smiles and kisses tasting like paan through the night, Gayatri woke up resolved, "I am going to start the day with a positive and uncluttered frame of mind, no x-rated thoughts allowed!"

Her father grimaced at her attire of faded pair of figure hugging jeans teamed with a threadbare sweater and took out some money from his wallet.

"Take this and buy some much needed clothes, Gattu. You obviously outgrew these in grade 8. Apparently they are not paying you in your new job as well. Henceforth I shall send you monthly clothes allowance," he grumbled.

Laughing, she took the money and said, "Thanks Dad, and make sure you send the money at the right time every month. But till I don't go out today and buy new ones, will have to wear these only."

Mrs Vohra hurried towards the entrance as the doorbell rang, hoping to intercept Nakul. But Gayatri beat her to it and ran to open the wooden door. Shocked at seeing Nakul there, she stood gaping.

"Happy birthday to you, happy birthday dear Gayatri," he sang oblivious to her dismayed reaction.

Closing the distance between them, he hugged her real tight and whispered, "Oh god, I have missed you so much, didn't know how much till I just held you in my arms. And as always, you smell fabulous."

Registering her prolonged silence for the first time, he held her away from his body and took in her expressionless face and immobile body.

"Are you not happy to see me?" he asked.

"What are you doing here, Nakul?" asked Gayatri, sidestepping to let him enter the house.

Perplexed at her attitude, he replied, "What do you mean what am I doing here? It is your birthday. I flew down especially to be with you today."

"I appreciate the effort you put in, but it wasn't required at all. I am sure you are extremely busy there. A phone call would have sufficed," she said.

"Don't tell me you are still hung upon my shift to Singapore," he broke off abruptly realising that Gayatri's parents had been observing the conversation for the past few minutes.

Greeting them both warmly, Nakul said, "I am starving Aunty. I was hoping for your world class aloo paranthas today."

Nudging her husband as a sign to give the kids some privacy, Neena Vohra said brightly, "Of course and I am also making chhole bhaturey; you know they are Gayatri's favourite."

Promising to devour it all, Nakul asked Gayatri if they could speak in her room.

Upon reaching the room, Gayatri said, "I am really touched that you came here especially for my birthday, but I wish you had consulted me before wasting so much money and time."

"Wasting? Since when has my wanting to spend time with you become a waste?" asked a now furious Nakul.

"This episode has been carrying on for weeks now. You refuse to grow out of your childish tantrums. The problem is not that I shifted to Singapore, but the fact that I didn't ask your opinion before making that decision. It happened fast, the timing sucked. So what! I tried apologising and making it up to you for that umpteen number of times in as many ways as I know, even offering to forego the most important career opportunity of my life – just for you. But no, nothing seems good enough for you. I made a mistake. Now what do you want me to do for absolution, beg?"

Gayatri was ill prepared to meet Nakul and his surprise visit had sucked the air from her lungs. She didn't know how to react and what to say. Nakul's barrage of hurtful words didn't help. She wasn't ready to confess her true emotions yet.

At her frozen expressions, Nakul shook her by the shoulders.

She flinched and said the first thing that came to her mind, "Please do not raise your voice at me. I think it's best you leave right now and we'll speak when you have calmed down a little. This is a request."

'So now you have turned into an escapist. When shown the mirror, you simply can't handle any sort of criticism about yourself, right? Fine, I am leaving. Am here till tomorrow evening and staying with Amar and Manav. Let me know when you are ready to come off your high horse and speak with someone who has flown thousands of miles just to be with you," said Nakul and left in a huff.

He made hurried apologies to her mother, who had come out of the kitchen hearing raised voices. Seeing Gayatri's ashen face and stricken expressions, she went and hugged her daughter without asking any questions.

After a pathetic attempt at breakfast, Gayatri pleaded a headache and went to her room. Her father followed her inside and said, "Why don't we go and shop for those much needed clothes for you and then lunch at your favourite Kebab Factory, what say you?"

"Okay Dad…" she started when the phone ring interrupted her.

Dreading a call from Nakul, she was relieved to read AK's name flashing on the screen.

"Happy birthday Gayatri. Hope you are having a wonderful time up until now. Err…I know this is a special day for you and you are with your parents, but I wouldn't have called had it not been so urgent," he said.

Mystified at her boss's serious tone, she asked, "What is it AK? Is everything in place?"

Aaryan, who was waiting for this very opening, said, "Well, there has been an unexpected development. Our client, Mr Maxwell has flown down to India for a conference just for the weekend and wants to use this opportunity to meet our HR resource who is going to be part of the project – which is you."

"But AK, I am in Delhi right now and I can't fly back at such a short notice," she replied.

He pumped a fist in the air and said, "Oh, did I not mention this – the conference is in Delhi and I flew down this morning. So if it's not too much to ask you, could you join us for a working dinner tonight at 7 p.m. at The Oberoi?"

Unsure of what to do, Gayatri told him that she'd figure out the plan and revert in just a few minutes.

Mrs Vohra asked curiously, "Who was it? What happened?"

Shaking her head, Gayatri assured her that all was well and explained the details of the call to her parents.

"It sounds important, baby," said her father.

Her mother agreed and told her to go ahead with the meeting, hoping that a change of scene would do well for her little girl. Gayatri sent a message to AK confirming her presence. Her spirits lifted at the prospect of seeing him in the night, but she ruthlessly squashed them remembering the look on Nakul's face.

She was feeling like the worst person in the world. Hurting Nakul was the last thing that she had ever wanted. She had been biding time in order to understand her heart and its complications before speaking with anyone else about it. But now that he was in front of her, how could she fake it?

Sitting in the cab, Nakul tried to calm himself. He had never lost his cool like this. They had had their fair share of disagreements in the past, but never before had he felt such primitive emotions. But then Gayatri had never been so unwilling or distant from him prior to this, which brought him to the crux of the problem. Nakul had always felt less worthy of Gayatri from the start of their relationship. But she had put him up on a pedestal, always making him feel extra special and giving him more credit than he deserved on innumerable occasions.

I have been taking her love and friendship for granted all this while. I had gotten so used to her agreeing to everything I said or did that I stopped caring about her views and thoughts, he thought to himself.

In the heated interiors of the cab, he kept recalling the sight of her unshed tears.

"I'll make it up to her. Let her calm down a bit after this argument," he told himself.

▼

Back from the lunch, Gayatri felt a little better and was glad that she had gone ahead with the plan. She decided to go through the project report once before the meeting. There was hardly any time left to get ready by the time she finished. She chose slim fitting black pants with a printed shirt and a black blazer. Gayatri kept the make-up to the minimum and pinned her hair up in a loose chignon. Wrapping an ivory silk scarf around her neck, she sat in her old car. She had missed driving on the congested roads of NCR all these months.

Aaryan kept checking his watch, impatiently waiting for his birthday girl to arrive. He had purposely called her earlier to spend some quality time before the client arrived. He looked up to find her standing next to the table. He got up and pulled a chair for her smilingly.

"I don't think I have ever seen you arrive so quietly anywhere, Ms Vohra. Here's wishing you a very happy birthday," he extended his hand warmly.

Gayatri was very happy to see him and her conscience was eating her up. Her guilt-ridden face gave AK a pause.

"Is everything alright?" Distress soaked his voice.

Touched by the concern in her boss's eyes, her tears surfaced. She tried brushing them away with the back of her hand and told him that all was well.

"'Do I look blind to you? Wait here for me," he said making a quick decision.

Gayatri sat uncertainly at the table. She thought it was best that she left because she was in no shape to contribute to the conversation. She needed to think of a way to speak with Nakul rather than run away from the issue. Till then, she *had* to maintain her distance from AK. His nearness confounded her, tempted her like never before. She got up to leave, but he came back to the table by then.

"You look decidedly pale. Are you sure you are not unwell?" he demanded.

"I, err…just can't do this right now. I am sorry for bailing out at the last minute. I know it's quite unprofessional on my part but…" he put an end to her babbling with a finger on her lips.

"Don't worry about the client or the meeting. It's been taken care of. I am taking you back home," he steered her towards the exit.

"What do you mean by taken care of? And where are you coming along? I have my car and I am capable enough to drive back. You need to go back inside and…" she trailed off.

"You are starting to worry me now," he gripped her arm and kept walking.

"And to answer your question, I called up Mr Maxwell and shifted the meeting to tomorrow morning. Now, can you please give me your address?" he asked

At her look of enquiry, he explained, "I need to give directions to my driver to reach your place from the hotel."

"I don't understand. Why do you need to come all the way till my house?" she argued.

Shaking his head, Aaryan said, "You must be joking if you think I am going to let you go back unescorted at this hour to your place. It is non-negotiable, so don't waste your breath."

Giving up, Gayatri rattled off her address while she started back for her house. AK sat in the passenger seat with his long legs cramped up in her mid-size sedan.

"So is it safe to sit next to you, while you manoeuvre the car in this crazy city?"quipped Aaryan.

She quipped back, "It was up until a minute ago, till you called my city crazy. Now I am not so sure. I mean, we north Indians have a reputation to maintain in front of you Mumbaites."

Seeing some of her old spark back in her, Aaryan breathed a quiet sigh of relief. He felt frustrated seeing her so distressed.

▼

Discouraged on receiving no communication from Gayatri till late evening, Nakul decided to text her and ask if she wanted to join him for dinner that night. After sending about a dozen texts and calling her a few times, he rang up at her place only to be informed that she was out for dinner. Miserable now, Nakul didn't know how to handle the situation. He didn't want this stretching to the next day. And so, he caught a cab and parked himself outside his love's house, whatever waiting it took. There was a fear gnawing inside him.

▼

The minute they hit the flyover, Gayatri let the car zip.

"What the hell are you doing? I can't see beyond my nose in this bloody fog and you are touching 100 kms per hour!" shouted AK.

Laughing for the first time in the entire day, Gayatri rolled down her window and let the freezing air rush in before replying, "Stop looking at me like I have grown horns. Have you never driven in such weather? I am a very safe driver."

Shivering against the cold in his fancy but thin blazer, he shouted, "*Safe?* You call yourself safe; no wonder Delhi has so much road rage. Delusional people like you are left to drive freely, making it life-threatening for your co-passenger and others on the street. And can you please roll up that window? My teeth are threatening to fall off any minute now."

Unable to control her giggling at his expressions, Gayatri complied nonetheless with the speed and rolling up the window, "See I have brought the speed to under 60 kms per hour and turned on the heater full blast, keeping in mind your middle age and health issues."

Their bantering continued till they reached her home. Gayatri got down and invited him to meet her parents. Aaryan got out while she parked the car.

Aaryan said, "I won't be staying long. Will just greet your parents and be on my way. I have an early start tomorrow."

Nakul couldn't believe his eyes. His Gayatri was gallivanting with someone else while he sat outside her house like a loser waiting to apologise for his behaviour. So this had been cooking behind his back. How could she do this? It had only been a couple of months since he had shifted to Singapore and she hadn't wasted any time finding someone new for herself. And to top it all, she was making him feel guilty about moving away from the city. Everything that he had said in the morning was absolutely correct, thought Nakul savagely.

As the door opened, she heard someone shout her name from behind. Pivoting, she saw Nakul walking towards her with a fierce expression on his face.

Gayatri took and deep breath and turned to AK and said, "I am sorry but I think it would be better if you left now."

Aaryan thought about protesting against it, but decided to go with her judgement, nodding his head in acknowledgement to her mother who had come to open the door.

Nakul reached them said, "So you two had a good time, huh?"

She looked at him steadily and said, "Hello Nakul, you have met my boss, right? He was just leaving. Let's talk once we go inside…hmm?"

"Why the sudden hurry? If I understand correctly, he was about to enter your house too, right, to continue the party? So why the sudden change in plans? Oh, I get it. It's because you didn't anticipate the old boyfriend coming to spoil your cosy twosome, right? Too bad. So why don't we *all* go in and have a nice chat?"

Before Gayatri could say anything, Aaryan intervened, "Look buddy, I don't know what is going on here and what your problem is, but the lady wants me to respect her privacy and I am going to do just that."

Thoroughly embarrassed, Gayatri managed to say steadily, "Thank you for seeing me home, AK. Goodnight. I'll see you at the office on Monday morning."

Hearing what she wasn't saying aloud, Aaryan shrugged his shoulders and turned towards his waiting limo parked across the street.

Before Nakul could say anything further, Mrs Vohra told him sternly, "If you wish to speak with my daughter, you will come inside the house and behave like a gentleman. I don't want to come in between your matters as you both are mature enough, but I would not tolerate any theatrics at or outside my residence."

A subdued Gayatri followed an angry but quiet Nakul into the house. She was relieved that her father had gone off to bed.

"I am sorry to have brought the matter to this stage. It's all my fault. I have been procrastinating all this while and I am afraid it's only made the matters worse. I have a feeling that I am going to hurt Nakul terribly tonight," Gayatri nearly broke down in front of her mother.

Hugging her precious daughter, Neena replied, "It's better to tell the truth than to give him false hope. I know you are very fond of him, but you have to be fair to the both of you."

Once alone with Nakul, Gayatri asked him if he had eaten anything or needed something to drink.

"Please drop this mask of your concern. I have seen and heard enough today to discover the real you," growled Nakul.

Crossing her arms, Gayatri sat down and waited expectantly for him to clarify.

Irked at her cocky attitude, Nakul said, "So you want me to spell it for you, is it? After feeling guilty about my harsh words this morning to you, I must have called you a hundred times, but to no avail. Still feeling the need to make up, I came and parked myself outside your house. I stood waiting in the cold while you partied and flirted with your Casanova boss. Apparently you couldn't wait to get back to Mumbai to continue whatever has been going on between the two of you. You absolutely had to meet him here, while on just a two day visit to your family. If you didn't find me interesting or moneyed enough for you anymore, all you had to do was call and tell me. At least that way I wouldn't have exhausted my time, energy and money to come here and make an ass of myself."

"I am glad you figured it all out finally, Nakul, and now that you have, I suggest you leave and carry on with your wonderful life while I enjoy mine," said Gayatri.

"No no no, you are not getting off the hook so easily. You need to tell me why you did it. Suddenly my devoted girlfriend fell for an arrogant asshole in a jiffy, who is more famous for his wild ways than his work. Or was your ego so big that you couldn't handle my not telling you about Singapore and you decided to spite me this way? *What was it…dammit…answer me?*"shouted Nakul.

Gayatri reminded him that they were at her parents' home and he needed to keep his voice down.

"Yes, I was to have dinner with AK and *no,* I wasn't flirting with him or vice versa. It was a business meet. As for your accusations in the morning, you were spot on about everything. I didn't like the fact that you didn't consult me about such a big decision and made me change my life as per your wishes. So I can't let go of that grudge. Under the circumstances, I think we should take some time off each other rather than dragging an albatross around our necks," she finished.

She knew she was being a coward in not confessing the truth about her not being in love with him. But she couldn't bring herself to do it.

"I will tell him soon… today he is in no condition to comprehend it," she justified to herself.

Nakul couldn't believe his ears. The girl in front of him was hardly recognisable. This was an unfeeling cold person.

"Let me get this right. Since you can't forgive me for my 'huge mistake', you want to break up with me? All that time spent, the affection, the words over the years have meant nothing to you?" asked a distraught Nakul. "Actually, don't bother answering. I can see the truth in your face. But let me tell you what I think. The truth is that you are basking under the attention being lavished upon you. I never took you to be such a shallow person. Unfortunately, you are nothing but a shiny toy for his amusement. I know you don't believe me now, but there shall be a day when you will," he broke off breathless.

Gayatri stood stoic in the face of this onslaught, but it seemed he wasn't done yet.

He placed an envelope on her bed and said, "Your birthday gift."

"It's an open ticket to Singapore…" he explained.

"I am truly touched, but right now, I cannot accept this from you. I know I have hurt you and am sorry, but I think this is for the best," saying so, she hugged him with a finality.

He was feeling completely bereft and left her house without saying another word.

Gayatri promised to speak with her worried looking mother in the morning and pushed her towards the master bedroom. She shut the lights and sat down on the bed only to get jarred by the ringing of her phone. She was surprised to see AK's name flashing on the screen.

"Hello, is all well AK? Have you reached?" she asked rapidly.

Aaryan had been worried sick about the situation in which he had left Gayatri behind and was happy to hear her sound normal, "Yes, I was just calling to check on you."

Touched by his concern, she told him that everything was fine and if he wanted to schedule the meeting for the next morning, she would join in. Though tempted to take her up on the offer, Aaryan restrained himself and told her it wasn't necessary and that he would take care of it.

▼

What has changed suddenly? In the past twenty-four hours, my life has turned upside down and I have no clue about what I have done wrong? thought a tired Nakul on his way back to the airport.

He had realised a few things that day – one, the thought of losing her was the biggest fear in his life and second, that he was capable of acute jealousy. When he saw that slimy multimillionaire place his hand on Gayatri's back proprietarily outside her house, it had blown the fuse in Nakul's head. Gayatri may be blind to her boss's intentions towards her, but Nakul could see that the man was definitely interested in her.

"And why wouldn't he be? She is as beautiful as they come and a wonderful human being as well," said a voice in his head.

Nakul knew that for all her shortcomings, she was perfect for his otherwise too mundane a life; his sunshine.

The first thing he did was to go to the ticket counter. He decided to get the ticket changed to his mother's name.

"I know why she is suddenly flying so high. When one is being pursued by a multibillionaire heir, it's easy to lose one's head. There is no way I am letting her go away from my life. This is just a small blip," he thought savagely.

▼

Aaryan tried to view the whole day's events as objectively as he could and the only conclusion that he reached was that he was the unwanted third wheel in this whole episode. He had mistakenly assumed Gayatri to be unattached emotionally. She was very much involved and her problems were hers alone. And that made it none of his business, howsoever desperately he wanted to play her knight in shining armour. Having reached that conclusion, he decided to stay away from Gayatri and her private mess. To hell with the attraction!

Gayatri had hardly slept a wink. She joined her mother in the kitchen while the latter prepared breakfast.

"I hurt him, Mom. It was terrible. But you know what is worse? I think he may be closer to the truth that I am. All this while, I thought that I was discovering my true emotions about him. But listening to him last night, I realised that this may be happening because of my…my attraction towards someone else. Oh god! I am horrible selfish person," she sobbed.

Neena didn't want to push her own conclusions towards her daughter. But she did try and explain that Nakul was upset and would say anything to ensure that their relationship stayed intact. What Gayatri needed to do was follow her instincts.

"Life isn't a perfect book. We learn new things about ourselves and people around us every day. In your heart, you know what you want. I want to tell you that I am glad you are not running away, no matter how ugly the situation is," she hugged Gayatri.

Rachna waited till Tuesday before calling up Nakul and asking him about his trip to India. Sensing his reluctance to talk, she asked him to come home that night as she was cooking his favourite aloo and puri.

"You have hardly spoken two words ever since you came in and you sounded cut up on the phone also. Is all well with you?" she asked, once they had finished dinner.

The warm welcome and attention acted as a balm to Nakul's bruised ego and he gave her an abridged version of his Delhi stay. From acute depression to immense happiness, Rachna felt she'd expire during the transition itself. This couldn't have worked out any better and was a signal from god that she and Nakul were meant to be.

"I needn't feel guilty about Gayatri's feelings anymore. She seems to have caught a much bigger fish; more power to her," thought Rachna gleefully.

Resting her hand sympathetically on his, she told him that he was being very wise and super understanding about the whole situation.

"Any other guy would have broken off with the girl right there and then, forget giving her more space after such behaviour. Gayatri is really lucky to have you…" she finished.

Flattered, Nakul now had a stamp of approval from Gayatri's friend. If another woman could see and appreciate his view, his Gayatri would also come around eventually.

▼

It had been two days since that ill-fated weekend and AK hadn't called her even once to discuss the new project or any other issue. Not sure about what to make of it, Gayatri decided to take the bull by its horns and asked Shweta for an appointment with him.

"He has a fifteen minute slot free right now before his next commitment, so why don't you come up immediately," said Shweta.

Not wasting another second, Gayatri went up to AK's office and knocked. On his terse summons, she walked in to find him standing exactly how he had been on their first encounter.

With his back to her, Gayatri found it easier to address the elephant in the room and began, "Before anything else, I truly want to apologise for you getting dragged in my personal mess and also thank you again for all that you did. I also want to reassure you that no repeat performance of the same shall occur ever from my end and I hope this won't affect the office equation that we enjoy….err, I mean share."

Cursing her slip of tongue, Gayatri waited as AK turned around and studied her face intensely before nodding his head and said, "You don't have to thank me or offer an apology for anything. As far as work is concerned, you know that I never let anything affect it. If that's all, then you may carry on. I'll have someone from the US team share the current status of the project and in case you have any queries, you can mail them to me."

Gayatri walked out of AK's cabin, determined to display her competence in her new role. She wanted to earn AK's respect as a professional and ruthlessly squashed her disappointment at the loss of their easygoing relation.

"I shall overcome this…I shall," muttered AK the minute Gayatri left his office.

It had taken effort on his part to control his happiness when Shweta had announced her presence. He hadn't trusted himself to turn around right the minute she had walked in. Searching her face for any signs of distress or unhappiness, Aaryan had had a hard time convincing himself to stay aloof and professional.

Knowing the truth about her sentiments being engaged elsewhere, he thought back to the conflict in his head while going back from Gayatri's residence. He felt he had made the right choice in keeping himself away from her emotional entanglements. She also hadn't asked him for any sort of help either; in fact, had repeatedly told him that it was her private muddle. This suited him perfectly as well. It wasn't as if he was looking to marry her! Now if only he could control his reaction to her every time he saw her, all would be fine. This was just a passing phase, a sort of softness towards the girl. It would go away; he would make sure of it!

The days became hectic for Gayatri as she immersed herself in the project along with the daily HR work. Apart from enjoying the new challenge which the project posed, there was frankly nothing else happening in her life. Nakul had assumed the role of a holier than thou martyr. He had sent a couple of mails filled with oblique enquiries about her boss and warnings regarding her blindness towards the pitfalls. She had tried replying civilly, keeping the interaction minimum.

Since coming back from Delhi, AK had reduced his interaction with her, which also suited Gayatri because he seemed to have the ability to get under her skin. It probably had something to do with his absolutely fantastic behaviour during that disastrous weekend. She wouldn't have given Aaryan Kapoor credit for the sensitivity that he had shown towards her.

I can't forget the time when he cancelled that all important client meet just for me and how did he figure out that I was upset? Lost in her thoughts, she got a start seeing AK in front of her.

Hastily she got up and said, "Umm...hi, you needed something?"

Yes, I needed to see you. Haven't seen you in a week now and I just couldn't stop myself any longer. With all these thoughts in his head, Aaryan simply said, "I haven't found time to sit through any of the conference calls recently, so thought would get an update from you, if this is a good time."

"You mean here, in my cubicle?" she squeaked.

Raising an eyebrow, Aaryan asked, "You have a problem with that?"

Assuring him that wasn't the case, she made space for him.

Sometime later, Aaryan leaned back into the chair and asked casually, "'So how is it going between you and your guy, err... Nakul, right?"

Striving for a neutral expression, Gayatri replied noncommittally, "We are trying to sort things."

"*That didn't go so bad. I have cured myself of whatever had bitten me,*" thought Aaryan, ignoring the racy pulse beating in him as he walked out of her cabin.

"Just ask the New York office to log me in the conference calls henceforth on the Maxwell project," he instructed Shweta once he reached outside his office.

▼

This was Nakul's twelfth call to his mother.

"Maa, what time are you leaving home? I don't want you to get late for your flight. Since it's your first time, you will take time to finish all the formalities. Just go early and wait there," instructed Nakul to his mother, who was coming to visit him.

"Only if you let me finish the work and last minute packing will I see you tomorrow, beta," she retorted.

"Maa, this is Rachna, Gayatri's friend and now mine too. She has been great with helping me settle down here," introduced Nakul.

Folding her hands, Rachna addressed his mother, "Namaste aunty. Hope you had a comfortable flight. I had told him to get you a day flight instead of a night one, but he thought you would have preferred the late night."

Liking what she saw, Mrs Shrivastava immediately pounced upon her son, "She is absolutely right. My bones are aching sitting through the night and I couldn't catch a wink of sleep."

Used to his mother's grumblings, Nakul grinned.

Moving to the taxi stand, Rachna said, "Nakul, why don't you go ahead and settle your mother in. I'll take a cab and go directly to work from here."

"But I thought you had taken the day off and were going to join us," asked a confused Nakul.

Having achieved what she had set out for herself in the first meeting, Rachna didn't want to linger on any further.

She said, "I think aunty is very tired and would like to rest for a bit. Why don't you go and spend some quality time with her. I will join you guys later, either tonight or tomorrow for lunch. It was lovely meeting you, aunty. Bye."

"Today he acknowledged me as his friend too. It's small but a start nonetheless. Soon, I'll be all that he would think and talk about," she vowed.

Reaching home, Nakul showed his mother the apartment and told her to take the room while he would use the sofa cum bed outside during her stay.

Seeing his bedside photo with Gayatri, his mother wrinkled her nose and asked, "How is your titli? That's what you call her, right? Has she been here to visit you yet or is too busy with her own career?"

He didn't want even a whiff of his disagreement with Gayatri to reach her because knowing his mother, she would pounce upon it and not stop till she made sure they broke up.

"Surprisingly, Rachna handled her well, or rather Maa liked her," he mused only to have it confirmed the next minute.

"She is a nice girl, this Rachna, seems grounded and sensible. Why couldn't you find someone like her instead?" she cribbed.

Irritated, he shot back, "Please don't start with the comparison or insinuate anything against Gayatri. She is going to be a permanent part of my life because I love her."

Sulking, she told him that she wasn't feeling well and needed to lie down for a bit.

Nakul couldn't stay in and went down for a stroll. He was angry with his mother. In agitation, he went ahead and dialled Gayatri on an impulse. It was 7 a.m. in India and seeing his number flash on the screen, the first thing she thought was that something was wrong.

Groggily she asked, "Hello…Nakul, is everything okay?"

Listening to her sleep laden husky voice, Nakul forgot all the recent past and said, "I am missing you terribly. There is a terrible void inside me. I need you. Come back to me please."

Wide awake now, Gayatri struggled to understand his words and said, "Nakul, tell me what is wrong? Why are you sounding like this?"

He said, "It's been hell without you for the past three weeks. I have hated every single moment. I don't want us to fight anymore. I am willing to really listen to what you have to say and follow it, but just come back to me, pleaseeeeee."

Her guilt kicked in. He clearly needed her and she had been causing him so much grief.

She heard herself say, "I have missed you too and I am sorry to have brought you pain."

It was like a dam had burst open and Nakul poured out his angst. They chatted like that for about an hour plus; international calling rates be damned! She put the phone down and wondered if she had done the right thing. Somewhere, her own loneliness had made her accept the olive branch that he was offering. She had missed the friendship, this familiarity and he *had* agreed to keep it uncomplicated. But she had a niggling feeling that she shouldn't have done this without telling him about her misgivings.

Aaryan's indifference in the past few days had made her question her own feelings – was she just attracted to him or was it something deeper? Her faith in her own judgement had been shaken. Was she fickle minded? Did she not know what her heart wanted? And what about AK? What did he want? So many questions… unfortunately, she had answers to none.

Over the next few days, Nakul and his mother ended up meeting Rachna fairly often. But he did not mention about his daily communication with Gayatri to either one of them.

"I think she is a very nice girl, Nakul. Now that I have spent some quality time with her, I found her extremely considerate. She helped me find places close to the lifts because I had mentioned about my fear of escalators. We went to an Indian place to eat. She also helped me pick things at bargains; she is not a spendthrift! I am telling you she is perfect."

A belligerent Nakul retorted, "Then why don't you go ahead and marry her because I can climb the escalator by myself and am capable of managing my finances."

"Why do you only look at superficial beauty? Rachna has displayed all qualities which are perfect for a sensible wife. Is it wrong for one to wish the best for one's child?" she uttered dramatically.

At the end of his patience level, he asked, "What if I don't want the best in the world but only the one who is best for me? Does my liking not matter? You had chosen jijaji for Di, right? So how come now you find so many things wrong with him?"

"Yeah yeah, I am the one always wrong in wanting what is best for my children. There is nothing wrong with her being beautiful. But why did she choose you? After all, to be frank, you are not the best looking of all, which leads me to the conclusion that she has an ulterior motive. She is looking for a guy she can dominate, the one who is so in awe of her beauty and charm and can become her slave."

Shaking his head at his maa's blatant attempts at coercion, he told her that Gayatri was his life. If she and his dad were to welcome her happily, it would make him ecstatic, else they could at least try to be polite to her for his sake. Either way, there was nothing anybody could say to change his mind about this.

Slowly things were normalising for Gayatri. Her interaction with Nakul was friendly and non-controversial. But he was pushing her for a trip to Singapore, almost pleading. She was contemplating it because she wanted to air out her feelings to him face-to-face. Her equation with AK had also improved. He was a magnanimous boss and a fair team player. Her parents were coming to visit soon and she was working long hours to compensate for her planned leave during that time.

Knocking on her boss's door, she opened it to find the ever elegant Mrs Kapoor with her son in the office.

"Oh, hello, ma'am… I didn't know you were here. I'll come back later," said Gayatri.

Happy to see her, Anjali Kapoor quickly replied, "No no, I was just visiting my son who seems to have no time for me these days. Why don't you come in? I haven't seen you in the longest time. Is all well with you?"

Aaryan had always believed that his mother would have made an extremely skilful interrogator.

"Heck, I have learnt more about Gayatri in the past fifteen minutes than I had known in the previous months put together. But wait a minute, why is mum so interested in her so suddenly?"

He asked Gayatri to wait outside his cabin for a bit.

"Now what is cooking in that devious mind of yours? You know that I do not appreciate any kind of matchmaking," he said.

His mother feigned surprise, "But why would you assume that I was trying to pair her with you? She is *so not* your type. I am thinking Gayatri would make a great match for Armaan."

Scowling at the thought of his wastrel, womaniser cousin, Aaryan asked, "Are you serious? You do know what kind of a guy he is, right? And Gayatri, of all the people? What is wrong with you, Mom? She is one of the nicest people I know and he is a jerk."

She put her hands up to calm him, "It was just a thought and if you feel so strongly about it, I won't suggest it to your aunt. But I find the girl really nice, so just thought she could be added to our family. Nevermind, I'll think of someone else," she added with a wink.

Irritated with his mom, he growled, "I am sure her parents and she are more than capable of finding a guy for her when the time comes. She is too young."

Mrs Kapoor was enjoying flustering her usually unflappable son, "Twenty-five is not too young by any standard, and nice girls like her are hard to come by. So if I were to aid in making a good match, I am sure her parents would be thankful as well. In fact, I am thinking of meeting them during their upcoming visit."

Aaryan shouted back, "It's not just appearance that matters, Mom. I have worked closely with her and there is much more to her than just looks. She has a razor sharp mind and a warm personality. She needs someone who can recognise and appreciate all that alongwith those stunning looks."

She hugged him and said, "I think someone already does."

She walked out of her son's office with a conviction that he was halfway in love with the girl already, whether he admitted it or not.

Gayatri had put up her parents at a hotel close to her flat as there was simply no place in that playhouse of hers. They visited

Mahabaleshwar, the hill station of Maharashtra over the weekend. Gayatri came back to work on Monday morning for a few hours.

"I thought you were not going to be working during the week," said Aaryan, bumping into her at the reception.

"I just came in to finish some last minute work; also I won't be joining in the conference call tonight, but if need be, just call me," she rattled off.

He grinned. "I know you think you are irreplaceable, but we shall manage without your presence for a few days. So just enjoy the time with your parents."

On her way out, Gayatri was surprised to get a call from Anjali Kapoor.

"Hi Gayatri! I totally forgot to inform you about the upcoming dinner at our residence for all employees and their families the coming weekend. Aaryan would be sending the mail today. Since your parents are in town, I want you to bring them along," she said.

Before Gayatri could react to the same, Anjali continued, "I also wanted to request you to aid my son in figuring out a suitable thank you gift for everyone for that night."

A bemused Gayatri mumbled her acquiesce and put the phone down.

Anjali had created this opportunity with a two-fold purpose – to provide her son and Gayatri an opportunity to interact outside the workplace, and secondly, to have a valid reason for meeting her parents.

AK called Gayatri the next morning, "Am so sorry that my mother dragged you into this last minute party plan. I tried telling her that it was your personal time that we were infringing upon, but she said that you had agreed to do this."

He mentioned the Bateel store located near office and decided to meet at the appointed time.

Standing next to AK, Gayatri said, "Can I share something with you candidly?"

At his nod, she continued, "I frankly don't like sweets too much; to top it, my taste buds are restricted to anything chocolaty. Dates stuffed with dry fruits don't feature on my list. So maybe I am not the right person for this task, though I didn't have the guts to say this in front of your mother."

At her frank admission, he laughed, "Yes, my mother can be intimidating sometimes, but funnily she seems to like you. And as far as *dates* go, you just haven't had the right one to appreciate it yet. So we'll organise a tutorial for you right away."

Not latching onto his pun, Gayatri just nodded her head glumly.

He held her arm as they waited to cross the road to reach the store.

To which she objected, "I am quite capable of crossing by myself."

Snorting, he retorted, "Yeah, I have seen the evidence with my own eyes."

At her look of enquiry, he narrated the incident about the day she had come in for the interview.

"Your crossing the road implies that everyone should just stop and wait for you to pass by, else they are all in peril," teased Aaryan.

Punching him with her elbow, she sniffed, "What a mean guy you are! I did no such thing and exaggeration is my forte, you shouldn't attempt it."

The store manager rushed to attend to Aaryan, his family being one of the biggest customers. AK asked him to get a sample of all possible types of the dates available.

"We possibly can't try all of them. What are you doing?" she whispered to him.

"Shush, what is your problem? You only taste the ones that appeal to you. I'll take care of the rest of them," assured AK.

Throughout the next twenty minutes, Aaryan simply gave into the pleasure of watching the expressions flitting on Gayatri's face, from tentative liking to outright disgust to surprised pleasure. By the end of it, he had a fair idea about what she liked and what not. Aaryan instructed the manager to pack only those sweets which Gayatri had appreciated.

"I have consumed enough sweets to last me a year," she moaned as they walked out of the store.

Used to her drama by now, Aaryan just smiled and headed towards her flat.

Her phone rang, flashing Nakul's name.

She asked, "Hi, am on my way back home. Can I call you once I reach?"

She disconnected the call and found a grim looking AK. Too soon, they reached her place and wishing her a curt bye, he drove off. She was upset and also a little confused at his reaction.

The same thoughts swarmed her mind. *Why do I care so much about whether he is happy with me or not? Why does the day seem brighter when he just smiles at me or pays attention to me? Why the hell am I upset just because he went away without opening the door of his car for me or wishing me a proper bye? On the one hand, he completely ignores me and stays impersonal* and suddenly he turns brooding and intense on me. What does he want? More importantly, what do I want?

"Mom, we are not going to spend too much time there. Will walk in a bit later than the designated time and leave as soon as decent," declared a determined Gayatri, still sulking about AK's behaviour.

"I am sure they'll feel bad if you did a hasty entry and exit," argued her mother.

They were at her flat on the day of the dinner, having come home to figure out the clothes for the evening, when the doorbell rang. Opening the door to a uniformed chauffeur, Neena Vohra received a huge parcel on behalf of Gayatri, apparently sent by Mrs Kapoor. Thanking the man, she shut the door and looked at her daughter with questions in her eyes. It contained the most beautiful dress Gayatri had ever seen with a note stuck on top:

A small thank you for all the trouble you underwent for me. Hope you enjoy the dress.

Jumping up and down with excitement, Gayatri put the burnt gold shimmering dress against her and looked in the mirror.

"Ooh Mom, it's fabulous!"

"It totally is and if Mrs Kapoor does it for all her employees, I must say she is extremely generous," said Mrs Vohra with a slight edge in her voice.

In the midst of strapping the heels on her feet, Gayatri looked up at her mother and asked, "Mom, I thought it was a really sweet thing to do!"

Her worldly wise mother reverted, "It is a sweet gesture, my doll, but I don't think it's an altruistic one. And I have an inkling... maybe she fancies you for her son."

Gayatri rolled her eyes and said, "Mom, just stop with the Mills and Boons twist. Do you know they are amongst the top twenty business houses in the country? You think they would look at a middle class ordinary girl?"

"Their business status and money power has nothing to do with it, and for your kind information, my daughter is far from ordinary," retorted Neena.

She hushed up her mom and dialled Anjali Kapoor to thank her for the gorgeous present.

The party had been arranged at the mezzanine level at the Kapoor house that evening and everything looked sparkling to Gayatri's eyes. Introducing her parents to her various colleagues and their families, she looked around for their hosts.

The console table in the lounge was filled with pictures and Gayatri looked at the picture-history of Aaryan.

Caught ogling at AK's pics, Gayatri felt her face grow hot under Mrs Kapoor's enquiring eyes. Apparently, she had cleared her throat a couple of times before also.

Anjali admonished her for walking in late and waited as she was introduced to her parents.

"You have a lovely daughter," she said warmly to Mrs and Mr Vohra.

'Why don't you go mingle with your friends while we 'youngsters' take care of ourselves?' suggested Rohit Kapoor, who had joined them.

She caught up with Taruna and Radhika, exchanging compliments.

"Red is definitely your colour," said Radhika, admiring Gayatri's off-shoulder knee length dress.

After chatting with the girls for a bit, she surreptitiously gazed around.

It seems that His Highness has decided not to bestow his august presence on his lowly subjects, she thought nastily, not being able to spot AK anywhere.

"Which poor soul are you abusing in your thoughts just now, Ms Vohra?" asked an amused looking Aaryan.

Irritated with him at having caught her musing almost accurately, she retorted impulsively, "What if I say it was you?"

He looked into her eyes said seriously, "Then I would say that I am flattered that you were thinking of me."

Suddenly the entire party vanished and left Gayatri standing alone with this man.

She spoke the first thing that came to her mind, "Why were you so abrupt the day before yesterday, spoiling an almost perfect evening?"

Dropping into a whisper, he said, "So I have the power to affect your evening, hmm? You wouldn't believe the reason if I told you."

Her heart hammering wildly, Gayatri opened her mouth to reply when a discreet cough reminded her that the 'being alone' part was actually a myth and they were geographically right in the middle of a party.

It was predestined, Gayatri thought as she faced the two formidable ladies wearing identical expressions on their faces... just had to be them! Rescue came from the unexpected quarters of her partner in crime.

"Why are you staring at me, Mom? Can a man not have a conversation with his HR personnel whenever he wants?" he asked.

At their disbelieving looks, he dropped his tone by a couple of notches and continued, "It's about a new project with a really big client; just that we haven't bagged it yet, so we need to keep it under wraps."

He changed tactic, addressing Gayatri's mom, "How are you, Mrs Vohra? How has been your stay in Mumbai till now?"

Giving the look of 'it's not over yet' to both their kids, the mothers walked away, one extremely pleased with the scene, the other not sure about what to make of it. With unspoken consent, they decided to stay away from each other through the duration of the party.

Burning with curiosity over what would have been AK's reply, she felt frustrated. There was no way that Gayatri could ask him that now! And then there was the scary pending conversation with her mum also. Oh damn, the party hadn't even started properly and fireworks were already in motion.

Not allowed to leave early, Gayatri and her parents were in fact few of the last ones to say their farewells. Hugging her warmly, Mrs Kapoor told Gayatri's mother that it was an absolute pleasure to be able to spend some time with her that evening.

"The Kapoors are very down to earth people," exclaimed Raj Vohra, having got along with Rohit Kapoor like a house on fire.

Finding both mother and daughter quiet, he realised there were some undercurrents afloat which he had missed, as always, and decided to look out at the breezy night instead.

"It was just nothing Mom; we had had a slight disagreement a couple of evenings before and I was only asking for an explanation," said a defensive Gayatri settled on the sofa cum bed at the hotel.

Giving her the 'mom' look, Neena spoke, "I wasn't born yesterday, my girl, and if what I saw was seeking explanation, then I wonder what a friendly chat amongst you guys looks like?"

Before her daughter could protest, she continued, "You know that I have no problem with whatever you decide in your life as long as you yourself know what you are doing. The minute I landed in Mumbai, you told me that things were not clear between you and Nakul still. Now I realise that my daughter has been down and out for the past two days because of some silly argument with her boss."

Bringing Gayatri close to her, she said, "We cannot sail in two boats, my child. I know you have had a rocky time with Nakul of late and I can see that Aaryan Kapoor is an extremely charming and attractive man. But you need to search your heart and figure out what is it that you want for real, because I know my girl is not into casual affairs, while committed elsewhere."

Gayatri broke down and confessed, "I have been feeling extremely confused these past few weeks and have truly truly tried to stay away from AK, but he tempts me like nothing else in the world. And the worst part is that I have no clue as to how he feels about me."

Taking a deep breath, she went on, "As far as Nakul is concerned, I can't see him in pain. I feel responsible for his happiness."

"Are you sure this is not obligation that you are feeling instead of affection towards Nakul, because I didn't hear you mention love anywhere, and isn't that the basis of your relationship with him? Does the thought of facing your real emotions about AK scare you?" asked a concerned Neena.

A disturbed Gayatri went off to bed, promising to think about the same honestly.

▼

"She is coming to Singapore!" shouted an excited Nakul, making people turn around and give him a look on the crowded Orchard Road pavement.

On his way to catch up with Rachna on Saturday evening, he was in for a pleasant surprise as Gayatri called and mentioned that she was going to book tickets for the long weekend coming up in two weeks' time.

"Of course I am free and more than happy to have you come here. Do you even need to ask?" he had responded.

The eagerness was spilling out of him as he headed towards the mall, wondering how the next fortnight would pass! The last few weeks had been good as Gayatri had come back to him slowly. Nakul was enjoying it more this time as he realised and appreciated her true value to him now. If he was honest to himself, it was only Gayatri and her support that was keeping him buoyant, else the foreign placement and the weekend partying had lost its charm for Nakul.

Rachna had adopted a weirdly proprietary attitude towards him of late. This had been one of the factors why he hadn't shared his current status with Gayatri with her till now, the other being he didn't want to jinx it by saying it aloud. But now that his woman was soon to arrive, Nakul wanted to announce it to the whole world, starting with his dear friend Rachna!

As he reached the porch, Nakul found Rachna getting off the taxi. Surprising her from the back, he went ahead and lifted her from the ground, giving her a spin in his arms. Shocked out of her wits, Rachna didn't know how to react.

"What has happened, baba? Put me down before I pass out in your arms," she threatened.

Complying with her command, he said, "I am very very happy today."

Replying, she said a touch drily, "Really, I would have never figured it out. Is it something at work? Have you been given a salary raise or wait! That new assignment has been given to you, the one you were pitching for?"

Vehemently shaking his head, he said, "There is only one thing in the world that can make this dry and ruthlessly practical guy lose his head – my sunshine is coming to Singapore."

When Rachna still didn't react, he said, "Oh ho, since when have your wits become so slow? Gayatri is coming down to Singapore in fifteen days' time and I am just going crazy by the thought of it!"

Unable to believe her ears, Rachna screeched, "What do you mean she is coming here? You said to me that she is in love with someone else and I thought you had moved on as well. So why… what…I don't understand."

He tried to calm her down and steered her towards the coffee shop inside. Making her sit, Nakul patiently narrated the incidents of the past month and wrapped up by stating firmly, "I never said that she is in love with someone else. I was jealous and there was a misunderstanding between us, but that entire thing is in the past now."

The ground became quicksand beneath her feet. She couldn't comprehend anything that he was telling her. Ever since his mother's arrival, he had displayed a significant change in his attitude towards her. He had chosen to include her during all interactions with his mother and even she seemed to have approved her. Then how can all this be happening now? This was a betrayal and just because 'Miss oh so lovely' Gayatri had seemed to tire of her toy-boy or vice versa, she wanted to come back to the stable and patient Nakul. But he wasn't hers to return to anymore.

"He belongs to me now and there is no way that I am letting go of him *ever*. So Miss Perfect can take her love and give it someone else," thought Rachna, almost smarting.

He looked at her, "Are you not going to react? Don't tell me you still haven't understood what I just explained."

Taking a plunge, she reverted, "You know you are very dear to me, right? Much more than a friend and what I am going to say now is for the sake of that relation, so don't mind my words," she started.

He reached for her hand and said, "I know you care for me deeply and I truly appreciate that. But I don't want to hear anything pessimistic about Gayatri or my relation with her. To be honest, that's why I haven't shared anything regarding this with you these past few days."

Rachna snatched her hand away and countered with sarcasm dipping out of her voice, "I didn't know you were the superstitious kind and that I brought negativity to you. If you don't want me to show you the mirror, then so be it."

With a huff, she got up and informed him that suddenly she wasn't feeling well and wanted to go back home. Not willing to invest any more of his energy in soothing Rachna's ruffles, he let her go. It suited him as well now as he intended shopping for Gayatri after getting to know about her trip and he preferred doing it alone.

Rachna brewed a cup of strong coffee for herself and pondered whether Nakul was worth all this heartache that she was going through. After a quiet introspection, she came to two conclusions – Nakul was a great guy and she was genuinely in love with him, and more importantly, Gayatri wasn't the right mate for him, no matter what he believed. Till now, she hadn't given much importance to Gayatri and her boss, but now she had to get to the bottom of things. Rachna dialled her number and waited for it to ring.

▼

"Radhika, I am trying to get in touch with Gayatri, but she is not picking up her phone. Where is she?" asked an impatient Aaryan.

"I am afraid she has left for the day already. She wrapped up her work early. Her flight is in a couple of hours. Was it urgent?" she said.

He frowned in the phone, "It can wait. I wasn't aware that she was travelling during these four days. Has she gone down to Delhi?"

"No, well she is going to Singapore to spend some quality time with her boyfriend," gushed an excited Radhika.

A belligerent Aaryan almost hit the security gate of his residence.

Anjali saw her son's car tyres burn as it came to a stop next to her on the porch.

"What is the matter, Aaryan?" she asked.

Giving her a thunderous look, he walked away.

Following him into the house, a concerned Mrs Kapoor reached him as he turned to go up the stairs, "Clearly you are upset. Won't you tell me, please?"

"This is absolutely the wrong time to speak with me, Mom. If I need your help, I will come to you, I promise… just let me be," said Aaryan.

Taking the stairs, two at a time, he went up to his now seldom used music room.

During his college days in New York, the Kapoor scion used to be lead guitarist of a band and an ardent follower of Kurt Cobain.

Now strumming it away in his sound proof room, he let the guitar soothe the frustration and angst swirling in his body since that conversation with Radhika.

"Has she been toying with me? So why does she give me those side-long glances when she thinks I am not looking at her and why in the god's name does she talk to me like my opinion means something to her, that I mean something to her? Why? Why? Why?"

Exhausted, Aaryan went towards his wing of the house. He stood under the hot shower, thinking about the way Gayatri had been behaving with him ever since they came back from Delhi. There had been warmth, respect and a hint of a little something more than care. But now he knew what it was… a sham, a pastime till her boyfriend didn't come back to town. With the world's prettiest chicks falling all over him, he had been duped by a nobody – an inexperienced girl with no social standing.

"I am not going to let her get the better of me. How dare she play with my emotions? She is in for a ride once she comes back from her love trip," he thought savagely.

▼

Sitting in the plane with nothing to occupy her attention except insipid movies and stale food, Gayatri's turbulent mind kept returning to the conversation with her mother. She couldn't run away anymore from the fact that she was more than just attracted to AK. Although she had a strong emotional bond with Nakul, it was high time she told him and herself the truth.

She had tried to speak with AK after the dinner at his house, but had failed to put her feelings into words. The conversation hadn't progressed beyond the office chit-chat. Frustration oozed out of her pores and there was nothing more she wanted than to run away from all this. But knowing it would only prolong and worsen the situation, Gayatri was headed towards one end of her two fanged monster. To ignore AK's calls at the airport had been a conscious decision. She didn't want to lie to him, but wasn't ready to tell him the reason for the trip yet.

She blinked as the overhead lights came on announcing their arrival at the Changi Airport.

Nakul waited impatiently for Gayatri to come out while resenting Rachna's presence along with him at the airport. Short of being rude, there was nothing that he could have done about it and now she stood scanning the crowd with him. As he spotted Gayatri, he ran excitedly to hug and lift her up in the air.

"You have lost weight, babe," he said bringing her back to the ground. Holding onto him, Gayatri tried to re-acquaint herself with his warmth and the feel of his embrace.

"Guys, I know you are very happy to see each other, but your love nest is blocking other people," said Rachna archly.

Gayatri went to hug her friend, a little surprised to see her at the airport at such late hour.

"Hey girl, I didn't know you were coming to the airport. It's really sweet of you to do so," said Gayatri.

Rachna surveyed Gayatri critically before retorting, "You do look peaked. Where is all that famous glow of yours? Left it back in Mumbai with someone?"

Gayatri looked at her quizzically, while Nakul reminded her, "I think now our threesome is causing that blockage that you mentioned. So let's get out of here please."

Nakul lowered his voice and apologised to Gayatri, "I am sorry sweetheart, but she absolutely insisted on coming along to meet you and there was nothing that I could do about it. But now enough, I am going to ask her to take a separate cab and head back home while we get to ours."

Shushing him Gayatri replied, "No, we can't do that. It'll look so rude. She came all the way here to pick me, we can't simply tell her to go away."

Rachna turned around, "If you love birds don't want me to hang around, all you have to do is say the word and I shall be gone. Anyway, I end up spending most of the weekends with Nakul, so I don't mind sharing him on this particular one with you."

Gayatri smiled but Nakul had a bad premonition at the base of his neck.

Ignoring Gayatri's forestalling hand, he told Rachna, "You are right, Rachna. I do want to spend some time alone with Gayatri, as you can understand. And I really appreciate that you came all this way just to meet her. But for now, why don't you head home and we'll catch up tomorrow for lunch?"

She gave a smile to an embarrassed Gayatri before signalling for a cab.

"Tomorrow then, at our usual haunt," she said to Nakul while getting into the taxi.

"That was very rude, Nakul," admonished Gayatri.

He responded by bringing his arm around her shoulder, "At this moment, I don't care. You are here for just four days and I don't give a damn for anything or anyone else."

On their way to his apartment, Nakul showed Gayatri the famous landmarks and buildings around. Falling into their usual camaraderie, Gayatri forgot about her confusions and worries till it was time to hit the bed. As she sat in front of the mirror, Nakul came from behind and took the comb from her hand.

"I have missed you and all these little gestures which make you so uniquely special," he said, gently parting her hair and running his fingers through them.

Gayatri felt no zing, no electricity course through her and tried to extract herself delicately from the situation.

"Are you ready for bed, my butterfly?" he asked seductively.

She turned to look at him and was unable to hide her dismay at his words. "What's the matter, Gayatri? You have been awfully quiet ever since we reached home," asked Nakul.

Cursing her transparent face, she looked at Nakul steadily before replying, "I think we are in the phase of re-defining our bond and I need to speak with you."

Nakul tried to kiss her resistance away, not taking her words seriously.

"Why are you acting coy with me? Haven't we been in this relationship long enough to forego this hard to get act!" he asked, a little annoyed.

After many months of celibacy, he had been looking forward to some intimacy on the weekend with her.

"You know I don't indulge in bedroom tantrums. I just feel we are at a disconnected stage right now, not on the same plane. We need to talk about this at length, please," she pleaded.

Giving her a knowing look, he reverted, "Which is exactly why I want to re-establish our connection at the most basic level."

A part of Gayatri wanted to test her reaction to his nearness. She let him drag her to bed and shower kisses all over her face. She closed her eyes, trying desperately to find that elusive link with Nakul. Instead, her mind took her back to the 'erotic pecks' of AK, which still remained potent in her head.

Disgusted with herself, she pushed Nakul firmly, "It's not working Nakul, I am so sorry. I just… can't do this."

There was only so much rejection that Nakul's ego could take and with a huff, he walked out of the room.

Going after him, Gayatri embraced him from the back, crying softly, "I am truly trying to find that bond back between us, but till then, please give me some space."

"I thought you had all the space that you needed for the past few months, but seems like it wasn't enough for you," said Nakul coldly and brushed her hands away.

Gayatri couldn't help but feel guilty about the whole episode. With her mother's words reverberating through her head, she had decided to jump out of both boats before she made up her mind about which one to sail in and sleeping with Nakul would've not been fair to her and him as well.

In the morning, she got up with a heavy head, only to find Nakul standing moodily in the kitchen.

Holding her ears, she looked up at him and said, "Forgive me?"

"You know very well I can't stay angry with you for long. Although I don't understand what is going on in your head, I don't want to fight over it while you are here. So tell me what is it that you want to do today," he relented.

Before she could reply, Nakul's phone rang. He ignored Rachna's flashing number on the screen.

Anticipating Gayatri's protest, he murmured, "I don't want anyone to intrude upon whatever precious time that we have managed to find for ourselves. So don't argue with me on this at least, hmm?"

They decided to get ready and step out for breakfast. Irritated with the ceaseless ringing of the phone, he just put the ringer off.

Gayatri dressed up in white shorts and a fuchsia pink tee with her hair braided, and put her gladiator sandals on. Her trademark bangles jingled as she walked towards him with the million dollar smile.

Pushing him to get ready as she was famished, Gayatri made up the sofa and puttered around the tiny apartment. Her phone rang. Picking it up without looking at the number, she realised it was Rachna on the other line.

"You guys have been avoiding me," complained Rachna.

Gayatri told her that they were stepping out for breakfast and would catch up with her after that. As she put down the phone, Nakul came out enquiring about the conversation.

"I told you that I want to spend some time alone with you, then why did you ask her to join us?" he nearly shouted.

Fed up with the attitude from both Rachna and Nakul, she gave it back saying, "You guys sound like a quarrelling married couple while I am the counsellor stuck in the middle. How was I to avoid her while she persisted? If you don't want to meet her, we'll simply not call her once back from breakfast."

"Okay alright, first breathe. I don't want to fight over her, of all the things. Let's just get out of here and then we'll see what we want to do," he replied.

After a sumptuous breakfast, they decided not to go back to the apartment and instead headed towards Orchard Road. Excited to be in the shopping heaven on this side of the world, Gayatri walked animatedly, trying to do everything at the same time. Loving her exuberance, Nakul spent the entire time watching the play of emotions on her face, until they bumped into some of his office colleagues from HMM. Nakul was bulldozed into sponsoring lunch for everyone. The merry group parted ways after four in the evening, after extracting a promise to party that night together.

"They are a cool bunch of guys and girls. I had a good time," smiled Gayatri.

"And I had a superb time because you had a good time," said Nakul, leaning in to kiss her on the forehead.

"On that note, do you want to go to the casino tonight?" he asked, knowing she would be thrilled about it.

"You better teach me how to play because I don't want to sit on those silly slot machines!" she exclaimed.

They headed back to his apartment to catch a few winks before the rocking night ahead. As Nakul crashed next to her on the bed, Gayatri lay awake pondering over her emotions to the various incidents during the past hours; from Nakul's admiring look when she came out of the room to his adoration while they were shopping to his pride in her looks while they were with his friends. She tried to evaluate her own reaction to these things and realised that all she felt was guilt, because every time she did something or saw anything new happening, she thought of how AK would react to it or what would he say to her in that situation.

When she had surveyed herself in the mirror that morning, the first thing that came to her head was, "Had AK been here, he would have given her that long brooding stare of his and said don't you think those shorts are too short and haven't you outgrown these flea market bangles yet?"

She realised that though she had been here physically, her thoughts were left behind in India itself with the man. Now she needed the right moment to tell Nakul about the same. She was dreading it.

They decided to go to the casino at Marina Bay before joining Nakul's friends at another lounge. Clad in a grey sequined short dress, Gayatri looked stunning. Having lost 50sing$ within the first twenty minutes at the roulette table, they hightailed from the casino and headed towards the lounge.

"I have been to this place a couple of times and it's the most happening lounge in town. You will simply love the music here," said Nakul.

As they proceeded to meet their friends, a hand clasped Nakul's from behind.

"Hi stranger," said a drunk looking Rachna.

Concerned at her inebriated state, Nakul took her on the side and asked, "What are doing here Rachna? You are sloshed; did you arrive here with someone?"

Words slurring, she replied, "Don't show your mock concern, Mr Shrivastava. I know better now. Just because your flighty girlfriend is here, you are ignoring your faithful friend."

Gayatri told Nakul to escort Rachna out of the place. Nakul waved to his friends from afar and indicated that he'll join them later. With Rachna draped around him fully, Nakul walked out with Gayatri following behind. Sandwiched between the two of them, Rachna put her head on Nakul's shoulder and started stroking his cheek.

"You know I like you, right?" she asked him.

Feeling uncomfortable with her actions, he said nothing.

Oblivious to anything, she continued, "When you wanted a shoulder to cry upon and listen to you rant about your girl, I was always there. And now suddenly, you are ignoring my calls, being rude to me and for whom – this girl? Forget loving you, she doesn't even know if she likes you anymore or not. While you didn't even look at another woman all this time, she has been happily sharing hot smokin' kisses with that boss of hers."

Stunned, Nakul looked at Gayatri, "Tell me that she is lying," he said through clenched teeth.

Guilt written all over her face, Gayatri could feel tears welling up in her eyes. Never in her wildest dreams had she imagined that her conversation with Rachna, shared in confidence, would come back to haunt her in such a manner. Stony silence prevailed in the car till they reached Rachna's apartment. Nakul removed the keys from Rachna's person and went in.

Nakul shut the door and came out to confront Gayatri.

"It's written all over your face, so don't bother denying it. My question is why? Was your love for me so weak that it couldn't hold onto the strings of a short absence also? Or did the lure of looks and money sway you towards that over smart boss of yours? What happened to the sweet and innocent image of yours that you project always, the naive one?"

"Let's go back home and talk, Nakul," started Gayatri, trying to calm him down.

"No one is going anywhere till you answer my question. Did you kiss him? And don't try to give any explanation alongwith; just a yes or no would suffice," he demanded, shaking her shoulders hard.

Gayatri whispered yes, covering her face with her hands. Unable to believe his ears, Nakul felt his whole world crashing around him. He fell down on the floor with a thump and as she tried to reach him, he stilled her with a look.

Pain etched all over his face, he asked in confusion, "Then why did you come here? Why did you spend all that time talking to me, re-building this relation?"

Words completely failed Gayatri as she saw him struggle with the twisted truth and she took the lashing in silence.

After a prolonged silence, Nakul lifted his head and looked straight at her, "I worshipped the ground you walked on and thought you could do no wrong. But I seem to have been the fool. Right at this moment, I want you to pack your bags and leave my house."

Gayatri gathered the tatters of her self-esteem and got out of Rachna's apartment to wait for him. She packed her bags while he paced outside his flat. Touching his face lightly as he flinched, Gayatri gave him a last look before heading out. Nakul screamed a shout full of rage and hurt when the door behind him shut.

Rachna came out of her room when both of them had left. She pumped a fist in the air. The wounds of uncertainty had been filled tonight by Nakul's shouts and all the planning of the past two weeks had borne fruit finally. Rachna was extremely proud of herself for that call to Mumbai. In her naivety, Gayatri had assumed Rachna to be her confidante – the biggest mistake of her life. Rachna thought her performance tonight was an award winning one because acting drunk gave her all the leeway in the world to blurt out everything accidentally without making her look bad in anyone's eyes.

"What would I give to be a fly on Nakul's apartment wall right now," she thought gleefully.

Gayatri made it just in time to reach the airport's washroom to throw up. The scorn in Nakul's words and the hurt of losing him forever ate her up. The journey back was completed in a daze and she informed her mother of her early arrival, begging her to leave her alone for a few days before asking for details. Curling up on her bed in her apartment, she went into a cocoon and didn't surface for two days.

The third day, Gayatri woke up with her parents threatening to come down if she didn't come out of the stupor. She assured them that she was fine and was going to join work the next morning itself. The guilt of causing immense anguish to someone so dear to her was burning Gayatri up from inside. Most of her life, she had been a people pleaser, consciously or otherwise and to see Nakul go through a heartbreak because of her actions, was unbearable for her.

"I don't know how to make it up to him," she thought miserably as she got ready for work. Thankfully Radhika hadn't arrived yet at her desk and it gave Gayatri some time to get a grip on herself and let the office work take over the sorrows and aches. Though Radhika remarked upon her appearance and low spirits during the course of the day, thankfully she didn't probe any further.

With work overflow due to the long weekend, Gayatri was grateful for the long hours and the relative oblivion in her cabin. The appraisal cycle was to start soon and she decided to get a jumpstart on it. It was really late by the time she got down to the office's exit. She stood on the porch trying to attract the attention of a taxi. Her attention was snared by a racy convertible that stopped in front of her. Honking loudly, the obnoxious driver, a hot looking female, tried to get Gayatri's attention.

"Do you work here?" she asked.

On her nodding, she ordered her to inform AK that his ride was waiting for him downstairs.

"Why don't you call him yourself?" asked an irritated Gayatri.

The woman replied, "I would if I could, but he is not picking up his phone. Can you go get him?"

Left with no alternative except being rude to her, Gayatri walked back to the reception only to find no one at the desk. She muttered expletives under her breath while going up to AK's office. Gayatri knocked, but got no response. She pushed the door open only to find it vacant.

"He is not here and I have been sent on a fool's errand," she grumbled and opened the door to go out, only to bang into AK as he was entering. Gayatri looked up to greet him. But the words died on her lips at the cold, almost condemning expression in his eyes.

"What are you doing here?" he barked at her.

She took a step back in the face of his unexpected hostility and stammered about the girl waiting for him downstairs.

"How considerate of you to come all the way up here just to deliver the message to me personally," he said sarcastically.

Tears sprang to her eyes at his harsh words and she turned to go away mutely.

He blocked her escape and pinned her against the oak door.

He tipped her chin up, "Why the tears? Fought with your boyfriend again? Looking for some solace from me?"

At his cruel taunts, Gayatri lost it and slapped him, "How dare you speak to me like that?"

Grabbing both her hands, he raised them above her head and lowered his mouth towards hers. Aaryan hovered over her tempting mouth for a fraction of time, fighting some inner battle before crushing her lips under his.

Gayatri's breath hitched in the throat and stayed there… time became immobile and eyelids dropped. Unlike the previous time, where he had caught her by surprise, this time she knew the kiss was coming and her body had been thrumming for it. Aaryan released her wrists and slipped one hand through her hair. He crushed the clip which had been holding her tresses in place. He caught her butt and brought her closer to his body. Gayatri opened up for him, letting him taste and explore her. With both of them shaking with the intensity of the moment, Gayatri's legs gave way and she sank on the decadent carpet, with AK not far behind her.

His hands roamed all over her possessively. He growled with pleasure, making her moan in return and her hands came up to touch and feel him for the first time. Running her fingers through his luxurious hair, she purred. Moving away from her aphrodisiac mouth, his lips explored her entire face, nipping and licking all the way till the shoulders. Aaryan bit gently at the base of her neck and blew on it. Her pleasured whimper made him bite her harder there. His exploring hands inched lower, while she sought his addictive lips, pulling his hair to get his attention. The shrill ringing of the phone brought them both crashing down to earth and not a minute sooner as they heard the pinging of the lift simultaneously. They sprang apart and got up hastily, her to reach for the phone in her bag and him to wait for whoever had arrived in the elevator.

Aaryan stood blocking the door as the lady from the car reached him.

"Do you know how long I have been waiting for you?" she screeched at him.

Raising an eyebrow, he looked at her haughtily, "I was too busy making out with a gorgeous woman on the floor right now, hence the delay."

The woman looked at him uncertainly. She wasn't sure whether he was jesting or being serious.

She replied suggestively, "I am glad you had a good evening. Now can you ensure I have a superb night as well?"

Aaryan shut the office door firmly behind him and stepped into the lift, keeping a tight leash on his throbbing frustration and self-loathing at the complete lack of control displayed a few minutes earlier. With Gayatri's body fragrance on his hands and her taste on his lips, he closed his eyes to savour the sensation for a minute before ruthlessly shoving it all away and walking out of the building.

Appalled at her absolute wanton behaviour, Gayatri came out of AK's office. Had it not been for the interruption, god only knows where they were headed. How would she walk into this office ever again without thinking of what had transpired between them? But as she went down to the reception, her mind started assimilating the conversation preceding the explosion between them. What had he meant by saying that she was looking for comfort from him and how did he know about what happened with Nakul? And most importantly, how could he walk out on her without a word to her after all that occurred here. Armed with all these questions, Gayatri spent the night replaying the scene in her mind. Next morning, she asked AK's assistant for an urgent meeting.

Aaryan looked up from his laptop, his expression impassive when she walked in.

She fumbled, "Well, I wanted to discuss something personal with you, err, ask you something."

Adopting a supercilious expression, he indicated her to continue, making her even more nervous.

"How did you know about Nakul and me having a tiff and what did you mean by your comment after that?" she asked in a rush.

Aaryan got up from his side to come around the table and sat across from her on the other chair, swivelling her to face him.

"I am surprised that you have come to me with this query. Don't you run the risk of it backfiring on you? Or do you think I am so blinded by your innocent act that I won't be able to see through it?" he snarled. Maybe this pretence of yours works well with that nerdy boyfriend of yours, but I have not been built from the same mould. Yes I agree, I got sucked into it once, but this time I can see through your conniving schemes. So whatever act you have brought to me today, I am *not interested*. If there is nothing else, please get back to your work, Ms Vohra," he finished on an almost violent note.

Gayatri sat there dumbstruck; the anguish caused by AK's venomous words was thousand times worse than what she had felt with Nakul a few days ago. With superhuman strength, she picked herself up and moved with lead feet towards the door.

"I don't know why you behaved the way you did or what is it that you think of me, but I am really glad that it has happened now," she managed to say before leaving his office.

Aaryan saw her stricken expressions and thought of going after her, but squashed the idea immediately.

Reaching her cabin, Gayatri couldn't think of a single coherent thought in her head and barely managed to pick up her stuff before heading out. Once she reached her flat, she gave into the emotions which had been threatening to overwhelm her for the past hour. By the time she resurfaced, the sun was settling in for the night. Staring at her reflection in the window, she tried to make sense of what had transpired that morning.

"Is this what he thinks of my character? How can he have such a low opinion of me? Was everything that we shared in the past a farce? And here, I thought I was going to begin a new chapter of my life, one which I wanted to write with *him*. But I was wrong. I seem to have disgraced myself in the eyes of everyone around me. I am done... with this city, its people, everything. To hell with you Aaryan Kapoor! *I hate you!*" she screamed.

The next morning, Gayatri got ready to take some big decisions, starting with putting in her papers at JBCN Corp. She owed the basic courtesy of informing Sudhir in person and went straight to his office in the morning.

Sudhir tried real hard to retain her, offering all kinds of help, but she didn't relent. He eventually gave up and asked her to begin the formalities. He rushed upstairs and interrupted a conference call to notify AK about her sudden resignation. Aaryan was taken aback at the news, but dismissed it as an attention seeking tactic of hers.

To Sudhir, he said, "I am sure she has some genuine issues which are unavoidable. Let her go if she wishes to and please start the process of finding a replacement immediately."

Perplexed at the day's events unfolding, Sudhir tried to figure out if he was missing out on something. He finally signed off on Gayatri's papers and told her that he'll be requiring her aid in the next few weeks till they found a replacement. She assured him all possible support and left the office without wishing farewell to any of her friends or colleagues. Next stop was at the movers and packers.

"Is she going to come back with a new ploy or simply going to wait for me to react," mused Aaryan.

"Because if she is going to wait, it's going to be a long one. If she decides to come and confess instead, I will consider forgiving her and maybe we can... no, what am I thinking. I am not going to show any leniency to her when she comes back. She has played with my emotions," he lectured himself sternly.

Gayatri reached Noida and told her mother that she was going to tell her everything on the condition that it was never raised again at their house. Haltingly she explained the entire chain of events leading to this nightmare that she was currently trapped in.

"I don't want you to tell me that it's someone else's fault or their loss. I just need you to be my pillar of strength while I learn how to sew back my tattered self esteem."

She continued in the same vein, "And do you know what is funny? It's only now that I am convinced that my feelings for Nakul were a combination of respect and affection. He would always be my best friend, but never my love. And the man that I wish to hate with all my might is the one that I have fallen in love with. Moral of my story is that the heart can be extremely dumb sometimes and does not act in one's best interest."

Days passed by as Aaryan waited to hear from Gayatri and with that not forthcoming, he asked Sudhir for updates on her. He was informed politely that she was still doing the back-end work for them on the appraisals and was acting as his support during the client calls for the project. Curious as to what game she was playing, Aaryan finally picked up the phone and dialled her number, only to hear the automated message of the number not being in service. He questioned his actions for the first time.

After a month had passed since her return from Singapore, Gayatri realised that she needed to stop mopping around and look for a job opportunity. Having worked at JBCN now, she had tasted blood and anything insipid wouldn't cut for her anymore. When the consultant offered her a similar profile in a start-up company, she agreed to go for the interview without a second thought.

▼

The ever pragmatic Nakul began to pick up pieces of his shattered heart by telling himself that it was all Gayatri's fault. She had misled him, cheated him and broken his heart. There was no way that he was going to allow her back in his life ever. On the other hand, Aaryan fought the battle between his ego and the fragile emotions that he felt for Gayatri. His misconceptions and insecurities won. He decided to concentrate solely on his work, shoving all thoughts of conniving females aside. All Gayatri could manage was put one foot in front of the other and try not think about anything or anyone else.

A year later

"You've got to meet the sexy HR manager. That's the biggest perk of working in this otherwise crappy company," advised Sushant to the new management trainee.

"Why crappy?" asked a nervous Veer, this being his third day of his first job.

He clapped the new guy on the shoulder, "I was referring to the miserly pay packet."

Slightly reassured, Veer said, "I am not looking for money but a steep learning experience. The campus presentation had been quite convincing."

Sushant grinned, "It had to be so. I was the brains behind it, with a little input from my boss."

"So how is she as a boss? Is there anything that I should be prepared with?" he asked a touch apprehensively.

"There is a long list of to-dos which she will hand over to you. But the only thing I have learnt in the past one year with her is accountability – to own up to one's actions. She is very particular about that," said Sushant.

Suitably impressed, Veer awaited his boss's arrival from Chennai where she had gone for a two-day conference on 'Best practices in HR in emerging industries'.

Cursing the traffic at Nehru Place, Gayatri reached her office a couple of hours behind schedule.

"In my office now, please," she summoned Sushant as soon as she reached her desk.

As her assistant manager walked in with the new trainee, she frowned, "I totally forgot about you, err, Veer Sahay, right? Welcome to Eternity Ltd. How is your induction progressing?"

Dumbstruck by her beauty, Veer stared at Gayatri for ten long seconds before finding his voice and mumbling a reply. Dressed in slim fitting pants and an office shirt, she sported no jewellery and had her hair pulled back in a severe chignon, showing off the contours of her face.

Gayatri briskly issued fresh instructions for Sushant before heading for an urgent meeting with her boss, Mr V.K. Malhotra.

The minute their superior left the room, Sushant pivoted and slapped the new MT on his back, "Are you mad? I told you to meet the pretty boss, not ogle at her. Thank your stars that she was distracted, otherwise you would've been out on your butt before you could finish saying boo. She is a tough cookie and doesn't tolerate any kind of nonsense."

Eternity Ltd was a recently formed company on the same model as JBCN, though at a much smaller scale. It had been started by Mr Sehgal, who owned huge ancestral farming land up in the north and had cashed out in the real estate bloom to invest in this company three years ago.

"What is it that he couldn't tell me on the phone or mail," mused Gayatri as she walked towards her boss's cabin, thinking back to the urgent summons that she had received.

"What I am about to tell you is not public knowledge and we wish to keep it so for the near future," said Vinod Kumar Malhotra, her superior and mentor for the past year.

At her enquiring look, he continued, "The company is being targeted for a hostile takeover by a group of wealthy moguls, and though Mr Sehgal is doing his best to find quick alternate solutions, we may see some management changes soon. It is imperative from our perspective that our data is accurate and up to date, ready for any analysis that the top management may demand anytime. There should not be any discrepancy in either figures or the qualitative data that we present."

Stunned at the news, Gayatri nonetheless said, "Give me and my team a week to audit everything and we shall be ready post that for any hurricane you send our way."

Smiling at her, he quipped, "That is what I like about you. You don't lose your cool under any circumstances."

She walked out, allowing herself a small humourless smile at her boss's comment, indicative of the long way she had come from that foolish, emotional girl to the now (hopefully) mature person. She squared her shoulders and started planning for the coming week.

"We'll conduct an internal audit starting this evening on all our databases and it needs to conclude by the end of this week itself. So please be ready to spend long hours at work. Before I hear a word of excuse from either of you, let me remind you, if we don't give out 100% accurate figures to the management, our appraisals shall reflect the same deficiency. So even if you don't value my instructions, I am sure you love your assessment rating right?" Delivering the stern talk to her team, Gayatri sat down to tackle her pending items before the evening.

Having learnt from the best, she followed AK's approach of being hands on, yet providing her subordinates the space and chance to do their best work.

The phone vibrated on her desk as she was about to get up for her much-delayed lunch break!

"Hey Nakul, what's up, long time? I was thinking of calling you yesterday, but just got caught up with something," she said picking up the call.

Gayatri informed him that she had been headed to the cafeteria to grab a bite.

"Some things can never change. If I am not mistaken, it's 4 p.m. in India now and knowing you as I do, breakfast still doesn't exist in your day. So essentially, it's the first morsel that you'll pop in your mouth and I can bet it'll be something unhealthy," he grumbled.

Smiling at the concern in his voice, she teased, "If you worry like a granny for every small thing, all that hair will turn white before you hit thirty. Anyway, what is new in your currently exciting life?"

He replied seriously, "Well, I am flying down to Delhi soon. I wanted to meet you before I head to Indore to see my parents. Dad has been unwell these past few weeks and I want to go spend some time with him. So, will you take out some precious moments out of your hectic life to meet an old friend?"

"Oh, I am so sorry to hear about Uncle, Nakul. Of course, we'll catch up. Let me know your flight details and I could pick you up from the airport day after tomorrow and we could grab a bite before you take the flight home," she asked briskly.

Mock angry, he said, "You have become a way better planner than I ever was, charting out my day for me within five minutes."

▼

"You are looking great, as always," he said, hugging Gayatri as he came out of the terminal.

She replied, "It's wonderful to see you too. Getting engaged seems to suit you."

Nakul shrugged and looked at his ring finger now twinkling with the diamond band on it.

"She absolutely insists that I wear it all the time," he said self-consciously.

To which Gayatri smiled and said, "Well, she is newly affianced, so you are supposed to fulfil her every whim."

Once they reached the hotel, choosing the buffet option, they settled down in the coffee shop with their plates piled up.

Nakul spoke first, "Dad is still the same. Doctor says it's mostly old age, but I didn't want to take a chance. As far as the exciting life is concerned, it seems that I am cursed to be around dominating women all my life, whether in the form of a mother or sister, or now the fiancée. So I am not really sure about the broth that these three are cooking, and frankly, I don't care about it as long as I am not dragged into it."

Gayatri said humorously, "I know, underneath all that cribbing, there is a very happy man lurking somewhere and that makes me very happy as well."

With a deep breath, Nakul dived into the topic that he had come to speak with Gayatri about. He could've chosen to do this conversation on the phone, but he needed to see her face expressions when he shared the news with her.

"I have a favour to ask of you," he started.

"Because of my father's health, the families have decided to expedite the wedding and they want to go ahead with it as soon as next month."

"That's wonderful news, Nakul. Considering you have known each other for more than two years now, I personally don't see any sense in waiting as well," she responded pleasantly.

His last flicker of hope died with her words, "But it also means that you have to figure out a fabulous wedding gift for me, which you will personally bring to the wedding."

Dismay flickered across her face and she replied a touch bluntly, "I would have loved to be a part of the happiest day of your life, but honestly, I don't want to cause any complications or discomfort to anyone."

"For once, I am not concerned about others' reactions or comfort. It's a big milestone in my life and I need you there. So you will have to come for *me*."

Why could I not reciprocate his feelings and love him like he loved me? No, I had to go and fall for the most inappropriate and ill-suited guy on Mother Earth, she thought morosely, after dropping him to the airport.

Gayatri blamed it all on the romantic fiction that had formed the blooming years of her life. She wondered cynically if it had been a mistake refusing Nakul's proposal a few months ago when he had come to see her in Delhi. Initially she had been reluctant to face him, but the fact that he wanted to move on with his life had given her courage to meet him and clear the air.

Nakul sat in the flight remembering his conversation with Gayatri for the first time after their break-up. His heart had given a leap at the familiar sight of Gayatri as she had walked into the restaurant that night. His hands had been clammy and he had had a premonition sitting there that his heart would never be whole again post that evening.

He could still recall her words clearly.

"Nakul, I know you have a lot of questions for me. You are angry and baffled at my behaviour. So I am going to tell you the absolute truth, one which I have discovered recently myself. When I first met you, I was an inexperienced but conceited girl who thought she knew it all. I presumed that a particular type of man was meant to be my soul mate, one with a focussed mind and an easygoing personality. You came in my life and I really liked you. You fitted the mould perfectly. I started to believe that I had found my ideal partner. But in this whole rigmarole, I forgot to account for a minute detail – my heart. And once I met AK, I realised that this stubborn organ could actually rule over all other functions in my body. I fell in love… for the first time in my life. No matter how I tried to convince myself or curb my emotions, it was out of my control. And much to my horror, I discovered that love is not clean or linear, but a messy emotion which has the power to turn one's world upside down," she had confessed.

"When I came to Singapore, I did not know that I loved him. All I could feel was confusion at that time, because being with you made me happy, but around AK, I felt alive," she had implored.

"That intimacy with AK just happened. The chemistry was too strong for me to defy and I caved in. The idea was never to cheat on you, but being with him had felt right at that moment. This is why I had flown to Singapore to try and sort my emotions fully before any of us got hurt, but in the end, I did end up damaging a lot more than I could have imagined," she had pleaded.

Nakul had given her a piercing look and asked, "You mean to imply that you have never loved me? All this time that we have been together, was just a phase in your life before you found your true love?"

Gayatri had tried to placate him by taking his hand in hers as she struggled to find the right words, "That is not true and you know it. You are and always will be very close to my heart..."

Nakul interrupted her bitterly, "But I won't be in your heart."

Before she could contradict his play of words, he continued, "So why are you here in Delhi? Why are you not where your newly discovered soul mate is?"

Gayatri's face had shuttered as she grappled with the pain in her heart, "He apparently doesn't reciprocate my emotions. It's now a closed chapter."

"But I don't understand. If he doesn't feel the same for you, then why are *you* clinging to it?"

Hearing his unspoken question, Gayatri had replied gently, "It doesn't matter whether my sentiments are returned or not, the bottom line is that I have those feelings for him. Anyway, at this moment, we are not here to talk about him and me, but for me to apologise to you for all the anguish that I have caused you. At the risk of a backlash from you, I still want to implore you to move on with your life. I truly wish that you find someone who appreciates your worth and loves you to the hilt."

It had taken Nakul some time before he could see Gayatri's point of view. Unable to sever his connection with her, he had reached out tentatively, starting with a casual e-mail to slowly re-knit the threads of their old friendship at least.

Coming back to the present, Nakul was surprised to hear the announcement of landing. With a heavy heart, he finally realised that *it* was over.

With all statistics double checked and battle ready, Gayatri gave her team a well-earned half day break while she waited for updates from her boss regarding their company's fate.

'There is no news yet, which means Mr Sehgal has been able to keep the wolves at bay for now. But I have been instructed to prepare a presentation depicting not just our numbers, but also our work culture and a detailed analysis of our employees' strengths and weaknesses," said a perplexed V.K. Malhotra to Gayatri.

To which she replied confidently, "I am aware of what the top management is trying to do. They want us to follow the JBCN way of evaluating employees. I was a part of developing that model and can easily replicate it."

He replied, "That makes sense. I had wondered about Mr Sehgal's request at that time."

▼

Gayatri took a day off from work to attend Nakul's wedding. Apart from Mrs Shrivastava's hostility and Rachna's veiled barbs, it was the sense of loneliness which made her question her heart's wisdom at the choices made by it in the past couple of years. Back home, Gayatri described the entire wedding with a touch of humour to her mother, exaggerating bits and pieces to hide her true feelings.

"Now that this chapter is finally over, do you think you are ready to move towards the future rather that living in the past?" asked her mother.

"Why are you in a hurry to pack me off?"

Undeterred, Neena Vohra continued, "I know that you had your first taste of love and it didn't work out, but life doesn't end there, sweetheart. Your journey has just begun."

Giving her a hug, Neena walked out of her daughter's room leaving thoughts for Gayatri to chew upon.

▼

"I need you to come into my cabin, right this moment," said V.K. Malhotra on the phone.

"You are one of the first people at the managerial level who is being informed about this decision and that too because we will need you to work actively on this and nothing else for the next foreseeable future," said Mr Sehgal, who, along Gayatri's boss, had been waiting for her in his cabin.

Considering this was only her third direct interaction with the company head in the past two years, she was extremely surprised to be addressed directly by him.

"In the light of recent attempts at taking over our company, we have decided to merge… with JBCN Corp," he announced finally.

A strange buzz filled her ears upon hearing the name, drowning out anything further that her CEO spoke.

"And since you are the only one here who has worked in that company and has a fair knowledge of their systems, I am putting you on the team which will plan and execute the hundred-day integration plan, which means we shall have these many days after the signing of the papers to align both the firms into one entity," finished Mr Sehgal.

The CEO looked quizzically at V.K. Malhotra, silently questioning Gayatri's dazed expressions and prolonged silence.

"What is the matter with you? What is it about JBCN that has rattled you so much?" asked a concerned V.K. Malhotra.

Hesitating a little, he continued, "You look as pale as a zombie. Were there, err... any harassment issues?"

Gayatri put a stop to her boss's wayward train of thoughts and desperately thought of a plausible explanation.

"No, not at all sir. I was momentarily shocked at the news. But if you could give me some details in terms of my role and responsibilities during this whole process, I'll be clearer in my head," she said.

Not convinced with her explanation, Vinod nonetheless started, "As Mr Sehgal explained, to save ourselves from the pack of wolves, we went ahead and befriended the tiger. Now the problem is that JBCN has buckets full of experience and ambition. Mr Sehgal's worry is that we shouldn't lose our entity in the whole process of the merger. He did manage to get us some breathing space in the hundred-day integration plan where Mr Kapoor in his arrogance agreed to negotiate the personnel allocation post the merger. Hence we want you to be a part of the team who will not only coordinate with the panel from JBCN, but also try and safeguard our interests during the process and people amalgamation. You and I both know it's the implementation that counts and not the contracts so much. And that is why we did not open our cards during the senior level dialogue in the past one month."

Seeing her fierce concentration, he continued, "What we have understood so far is that JBCN wants to retain our business development team, but not our operations guys. But Mr Sehgal believes that it is the successful implementation that has sustained us so far and we have grown as a company. So he wants to retain his star project managers. As far as your role is concerned, the truth is, you are our only vantage point into their working style and thought process."

At her look of protest, Vinod clarified, "We are not expecting you to go break into their vault, but to use your experience with that company to secure the best deal possible for Eternity Ltd at every level, whether it is placing our employees in a particular role, or to set up procedures and policies at the corporate level which are beneficial to us."

Finally out of Vinod's cabin, Gayatri took deep breaths willing her galloping heart to calm down.

"So much for my newfound maturity and self-control," she snorted in disgust.

Reaching her desk, Gayatri wrote a hasty mail to her team, leaving instructions for the rest of the day and left office. Driving aimlessly, she entertained the thought of quitting seriously before discarding it.

"Why should I leave my workplace just because there is a probable meeting with his Royal Highness in the near future? I have committed no crime and if he finds my presence unpalatable, then that would be his problem and he can throw me out if he wishes. But he can't make me run away before that," she lectured herself.

It was late in the evening when she parked on the front porch of her house; shutting the engine, she debated telling her parents about the new development, but decided against it for now.

▼

She had been instructed to shift to the project managers' level for the entire duration of the merger process. Praying for strength and guidance, she went up to the 6th floor, where her new workstation had been put up. There were four members in the team, including Rahul Chaddha, representing the business development group. Good looking in a slick way, he had been enamoured with Gayatri ever since she joined the firm and had refused to take her repeated hints about not being interested in any sort of liaison with him. Inwardly groaning at their increased future interactions, Gayatri maintained a neutral facade while greeting everyone. Except her, they were all at senior manager level and brought in a lot more experience with them.

"This is a sign from heaven that we are meant to be together," whispered Rahul at the first possible opportunity to Gayatri.

She turned to look at him fiercly, "In the interest of our working together, I am going to say this just once – back off!"

Without waiting for his reaction, she walked away in the direction of the coffee station. From persistent lecherous suitors to nasty Greek gods, she was already feeling overwhelmed and the games hadn't even begun yet!

▼

"Is the deal signed and sealed, Aaryan?" enquired Rohit Kapoor.

"It will take a few more days, dad. I am planning to fly down by the end of the week with the lawyers to take care of the details. But the critical part is the fortnight after the merger is announced when the initial bit of negotiations start. Once that goes smoothly, which I assume it would, we'll be back to business as usual; though with a whole gamut of cash rich mid-sized clients in our portfolio," he grinned.

Mr Kapoor nodded his head and recalled their conversation at the beginning of the merger, "Why did you not take over the business, instead of going this way? I know we have the muscle and the influence to easily achieve that."

Aaryan had replied, "Yes, you are right, we can do that. But the truth is that this is a faster process to achieve our end goal – increase our presence in the country. Without incurring the extra cost in buying everything out, I shall have an established unit, and since we are the bigger partners, we shall get the systems and processes running the way we want. So how is it any different from a takeover? In fact, it is friendlier and they'll be bending backwards to accommodate us."

With a word of caution about not underestimating the smaller company, his father had dropped the topic that time.

Coming back to the present, he treaded cautiously as he picked another topic to discuss with his son, one which his wife had been nagging him about.

"I was, uh… wondering if you were free tonight to catch up for dinner with an old friend of mine and his family," started Rohit Kapoor.

AK pondered for a minute before replying nonchalantly that he would be happy to do so.

"Your mother has asked them over to our place. So I'll see you at home around eight," he replied. The stress of managing a large corporate empire was nothing in comparison to the pressure of carrying out his wife's commands perfectly, he thought ruefully.

At the end of a boring evening with the clingy father and a clingier daughter, the Kapoor family was ready to pull each other's hair out.

"What a colossal waste of time!" muttered an irritated Anjali Kapoor.

"Considering it was your brilliant plan at matchmaking for me, I would completely agree with you, dear mother," replied an amused AK to his now thoroughly peeved mom.

He looked at both his parents and told them earnestly, "When I feel the need to get married and am not able to find a suitable partner for myself, I promise you'll be the first ones to know. But as of now, I am happily single."

Sniffling, Mrs Kapoor retorted, "Of course you are. With a new arm candy every week, I am sure your father also must be getting jealous of you. But are you not beginning to get tired of the whole charade now?"

The last statement was asked in all innocence by his mother, which didn't fool him for even a bit. Pointing a finger at her, AK told her that he was aware of her tactics and next time if she wanted something out of him, she wasn't to include his poor father and come to him directly.

"Sudhir, you are going to be our focal point here along with the chosen people of Contacts (SPOCs) from the business development team, accounts and, of course, the operations team. Radhika can take care of the work here while you handle the HR bit in the new merged entity. It is very important that we get our style of functioning set up right from the word go. I need you to handle the HR representative there politely but firmly. I have met him once and he seems to be quite agreeable," instructed AK the next day at work.

Sudhir responded amiably, "I don't foresee any major issues, AK. The appraisal that we had asked them to do for their entire organization a few weeks ago, was in sync with our method and was surprisingly completed before time. At least the HR team seems extremely efficient over there."

To which AK reacted quickly, "Then make sure you retain some of them in the new company. We are always in need of good people and I am sure the chosen ones will be happy to come on board instead of being handed the pink slips."

Recalling a particular set of mischievous hazel eyes, AK got hit by unexpected nostalgia sitting right there in his office, with a longing so fierce that it left him breathless for a bit.

He spoke brusquely to Sudhir, "Why don't you get in touch with the assigned people today itself? It is Wednesday, we still have three working days this week, if we include Saturday. So let's start the negotiations right away. There is no need to wait till the next week when I fly down to join you. I am off to Hyderabad for a few days to meet a prospective client. Surely you'll have everything in control by the time I return."

Once Sudhir left his office, AK gave a stern dressing down to himself, "If she is going to keep popping up in my head every time I hear someone say HR, I'll never be rid of her memories. Her elusive smell, those luminous eyes and her infectious laugh keep haunting me."

Gayatri did not know what would be the reaction from the JBCN boss once they knew it was her on the other side of the fence – whether he would be his vindictive self and ask for her resignation or would he be indifferent and ignore her presence. Either way, she was ready for any outcome and her pragmatic side told her that being part of a merger process would enhance her resume multifold. So keeping her emotions aside, Gayatri concentrated on her work.

"The JBCN team is flying down tomorrow morning and we'll sit for negotiations 11 a.m. onwards in the conference room on the CEO floor," announced the operations manager.

Gayatri went to Vinod's cabin right after the declaration and reiterated to him, "You are going to be sitting in the meeting, while I'll be here in your office waiting for any query or clarification, as per our plan."

It had been Gayatri's idea to stay away from the limelight as she thought they would lose their slight edge of surprise if JBCN discovered her presence at this stage and decided to bar her from taking part in the proceedings.

"You know whatever we can swing our way shall be decided within the next week or so, and it's very important we bombard them early on when they are not expecting it from us," stressed Vinod.

"So the JBCN team comprises Sudhir Mishra, Vikram Behl for ops, Taruna from BD and Kamath from accounts. Who all do you know out of these?" asked Vinod.

With a wistful smile, she said, "All of them have been my good friends in the past and Sudhir was my mentor and guru and most of my current working knowledge has been imparted by him. To tell you the truth, I am feeling a little bad about this whole cloak and dagger situation now."

Patting her shoulder, Vinod reminded her that they were doing what was best for the company and there was no personal agenda involved. Gayatri shied away from thinking about her personal reasons for evading the confrontation for as long as possible.

▼

"I don't think this should take long as most of the areas were covered under the hundred-days integration plan," started Sudhir in the conference room at Eternity.

Vinod countered smoothly, "Of course, but we wanted to begin today by highlighting a few improvements. The current process that is employed by JBCN from procuring the client to finally handing over the business back to them is divided into four stages."

Saying so, he put on the first slide on their PowerPoint presentation which depicted the above-mentioned method.

"We at Eternity follow almost the same pattern, except for one little addition – we have an active presence in our client's business for the next six months after the handover is done, ensuring high client satisfaction. In the process, our project managers are able to pick up in-depth knowledge and sometimes new skill sets, enabling us to pitch for new business in related sectors as well. It also ensures positive feedback from the current client since this service is charged nominally and weeds out any lingering hiccups existing post the handover. And adding this bit to our process has ensured repeat business and long term clients to Eternity. The data has been highlighted for your reference. We strongly feel that in the new company, this should be incorporated," he finished.

Caught napping at the boundary, Vikram and Sudhir scrambled to look at the figures which had been provided. Even after shredding the data to bits, the final conclusion weighed in favour of including the given suggestion. At the end of the day, as team Eternity filed out of the conference room, Sudhir and the others went into a huddle in that conference room itself.

"This was an ambush. It's clear now that they have studied our processes and systems in and out and in our arrogance as a superior partner, we came totally unprepared. And something tells me that this is just the beginning; so the question arises – do we bring AK in right away or wait for another day?" asked a worried Taruna.

"There is no doubt that he needs to be updated immediately. He won't like the fact that a newbie company has shown errors in our well-established processes and that also backed with data. I'll do a teleconference with him later tonight. We need to be fully prepared for tomorrow. So let's try and identify the areas that they can hit us upon," instructed Sudhir.

▼

Amidst the excited chatter in Vinod's office, Mr Sehgal tried to calm everyone down by saying that this was only the start and that the other side would be wary and better equipped now onward.

"So please get back to your workstations and let's stick to the plan," he instructed all five of them.

"What is the meaning of all this? In the first place, is this data accurate? Secondly, why have we not studied their company policies and systems in-depth? And how did they get such detailed access to our workings? I need these answers and we need to develop a strategy fast to counter them because I am sure this is not a one off event," AK bellowed on the phone.

Sudhir tried to reassure him that they would start working right away on all matters of concern. AK informed them that instead of next Friday, he would fly down on Tuesday itself. But that was still four days away and they needed to keep it under control till then.

Pacing in his hotel suite in Hyderabad, Aaryan Kapoor wondered about the motive behind today's ploy and the people responsible for the same.

"When I had met the top level executives during the merger talks, none of them seemed sharp enough to come up with this. I may have been wrong, but they all looked to be extremely compliant and in fact a little intimidated when I had addressed them personally. So who is causing this little niggle in my plans," mused Kapoor Jr.

▼

"Good morning everyone, after a detailed discussion with our CEO yesterday, we have been advised to consider your proposal about the process change. So now if there is nothing else, we would like to start discussing the salary structure across levels and freeze those today itself," started a slightly hostile Kamath, the accounts head from JBCN.

The day progressed with Eternity agreeing to almost all the suggestions put forth by JBCN. Sudhir and his team relaxed and were almost jovial when they reconvened after lunch for the next round. It was the turn to discuss the operations managers and their salary structure.

"Before you begin, let me tell you that we are happy to adopt any and all salary related suggestions that you have across levels. The same has been conveyed by Mr Sehgal himself. But we do have a small request to make," said Vinod, with a smile.

Vinod stood up and started the projector depicting a number laden matrix on the screen.

"This looks interesting, but what is it?"asked Vikram.

'This is the performance chart of our star operations managers who have delivered on all parameters of evaluation, repeatedly and consistently. As you can see, we have mapped them on various parameters, ranging from technical to managerial to soft skills. Unlike your organization where one manager takes care of one client deal at a time, our managers overlook three-four projects at a go and have been able to deliver on all of them effectively till now. I am aware that our discussion on people allocation has not started yet, but I just wanted to give a heads-up and provide you with all the relevant figures for a well-informed decision on the same. I am sure that you have mapped your employees on the same parameter as well, but this way we'll get a fair comparison of all managers uniformly. Also, our appraisal cycle is a continuous process through the year, rather than a yearly event. Hence the data which we have provided is real time," he said

The JBCN team realised that they had been duped again and very cleverly, by these sneaky b********.

"AK is going to cream us on this one totally," muttered Taruna morosely.

▼

Rahul Chaddha excitedly clapped Prateek's shoulder standing at the coffee station and said, "Gayatri is totally amazing, isn't she! I swear I am going to propose to her right after these negotiations are over."

They both failed to notice the presence behind them, someone who had been at the far end, next to the water cooler, partially obscured by the vending machines.

▼

"What exactly are you guys doing there? How did my handpicked team get beaten by a newbie company's people *again*? And what are the merits of this ongoing appraisal system? Why hasn't it been presented to me yet by my own HR team?" hissed Aaryan on the phone.

A troubled Taruna started tentatively, "I may have some inkling about what is going on, but the accuracy of this information has not been validated."

He nearly shouted in the phone, "Just say it without any melodrama please."

"I think Gayatri is working in that organization," she blurted out.

Complete silence prevailed at both ends of the phone line as everyone tried to digest this startling news.

Sudhir was the first one to break the silence as he started slowly, "I need to know how you came by this information."

As Taruna narrated how the men had not seen her as they spoke, AK was convinced as soon as he heard about Rahul Chaddha's comments.

"It's definitely her," said AK through gritted teeth.

Sudhir asked their boss, "So what are we going to do about it now?"

On the third day of negotiations, Gayatri walked in with a big smile for her old friends. She went and shook hands with her mentor warmly. She hugged Taruna tight with eyes tearing up of their own accord.

"How are you Vikram, Mr Kamath?" she asked as Vikram hugged her as well and Mr Kamath greeted her politely.

"You have been a naughty girl, Gayatri!" admonished Vikram.

Choosing a chair midway, she began earnestly, "Before you chastise and punish me, I want to tell you something upfront.

"There was a valid reason why we went this way. In all honesty, had we used the normal means of putting forth the requests, they would have been shot down immediately by the bigger and more powerful JBCN," she stressed.

Waving down the look of protest from Taruna, she continued, "Till now, we at Eternity, have not asked for anything which is not in the interest of the new company. It was done this way for you to take notice of these issues seriously and I promise you there was no other ulterior motive, which is why I have come out in the open today and shared all this with you. No more games henceforth, I promise.

Everyone looked at Sudhir for his reaction.

Looking at his protégée, Sudhir simply said, "Nicely done! Just because I am fond of you doesn't mean you are going to get off trouble-free. In fact, I am going to make you pay for all the difficulty you put us in with AK."

A collective sigh of relief was audible in the Eternity camp.

"We may have a problem. Just step out with me for a minute," murmured Vinod urgently to Gayatri.

Giving him a questioning look, she got distracted by Vikram, who delved into the discussion of one of the best practices being followed at JBCN. Gayatri responded with equal heat and passion, not aware of the pin-drop silence which had fallen into the room. Suddenly she stopped mid-sentence as the reason for the same came and stood in front of her.

"Just what are you up to, Ms Vohra?" said a quietly seething Aaryan, as he entered the room with Mr Sehgal.

Aware of everyone's eyes on them, Gayatri fought hard to keep up her outwardly calm as her stupid heart beat drums at the arrival of its long lost owner.

"How are you, AK? As for your question, I am just doing my job," she replied, proud of no visible tremor in her voice.

Crossing over to the far end of the round table, he said, "I know your love for games. But I don't appreciate being made a pawn in them."

Vinod attempted to intervene, only to be silenced by a severe look from AK.

"You were fully aware of all the facts when you consciously chose to follow the path of deceit and it didn't matter to you who or what would be affected in the process. But enough is enough, it's time that someone put a stop to your pretence," he said with barely suppressed rage.

"You need to calm down AK," said Sudhir softly, sliding up to him.

Shaken to the core, Gayatri hadn't thought that AK would be so angry with her.

Finally Vinod got up and said, "It wasn't Gayatri's personal decision, nor was there any dire intention on any of our parts. The same has been explained to your team in detail already this morning, Mr Kapoor."

Pushing back his chair, Aaryan drew up to his full height before smiling sardonically and addressing Gayatri, "You seem to always have a bunch of loyalists hanging around you, ready to defend you so earnestly."

Fed up of his high-handed attitude, Gayatri got up and shot back, "Sir, if you have anything to say to me, please say it directly to my face."

"I am really really glad to see you after ages. Haven't felt this alive in years now; my whole body is strumming like an in-tune guitar." With all these words at the tip of his tongue, Aaryan took his eyes off Gayatri for the first time, since entering the room.

"I think we are all over-reacting with all the stress and anxiety of the past weeks catching up, so let's all take a break and re-convene within an hour or so," said Sudhir, placing a restraining hand on AK's arm.

Everyone including Mr Sehgal moved out, leaving Gayatri and AK standing along with Sudhir in the room.

"Whatever differences that you may have with each other, please remember this is neither the time nor the place to air it," he said and left the room.

Two pairs of hungry eyes took measure of all the changes they could discern after a long gap of one year.

How can he look this good, while I am in the middle of a nervous breakdown? she thought eyeing him grumpily.

Taking a deep breath, she plunged in first, "I apologise for the way we presented our case, but as I explained to Sudhir earlier today, knowing JBCN and you, there was no other way to get your attention. The intention was never to dupe anyone, but make an impact so that the right data is presented in the most effective manner."

After waiting a beat, Aaryan said, "That's it? You have nothing to say for your Houdini act in the past 13 months."

Eyes smouldering, she replied, "I wasn't aware that you were looking for me."

She walked out without a backward glance, only to crash into Rahul outside the door.

"You don't need to look for excuses to hug me," he winked at her.

Yanking herself away from him, she muttered furiously, "Are you dumb? Don't you know when a woman says no to you and means it?"

AK materialised next to her and ushered her away from the door wordlessly. She stood frozen by the unexpected contact before brushing his hand and walking away.

"This will not work. I thought I had it all planned out, but seeing him in flesh today…. I forgot everything and let him touch me. That hand caused goose-bumps to break out all over my body like a bad rash. If this is my reaction when he had humiliated me, then it will be catastrophic the minute he decides to behave normally with me," she conducted the monologue in her head.

▼

"What is wrong with you, AK? I haven't seen you lose control like this ever. This behaviour is not appropriate for the CEO of a newly merged company, especially in front of people who barely know you," chided Sudhir.

Furious with himself for getting a brain freeze the minute he saw Gayatri, he was embarrassed as he recalled how he had nearly given away his true feelings. The only silver lining in the whole episode was that she was nearly as badly rattled, if her flushed face was an indicator.

"Are you alright? I asked you a question and you are smiling to yourself, looking vacantly in the air for the past five minutes," asked a worried Sudhir.

"I thought we had decided last night that as of now I would be handling the confrontation with Gayatri and you would step in later, if need be," commented Sudhir as a parting shot, not expecting an answer from AK.

"I couldn't stay away, knowing she was here – back in my company," he murmured.

▼

A guilt ridden Vinod said, "My apologies to you. I didn't anticipate Mr Kapoor getting so angry and end up blaming you for everything while we sat back as mute spectators."

Shrugging it off, she assured him that she had a word with AK and all was in order now.

"Good job done on the merger bit! Now you can resume your regular responsibilities," praised Vinod.

A relieved Gayatri left his cabin.

"Now that the air has been cleared, let's start afresh," Vinod offered an olive branch to the JBCN team.

"Shouldn't we wait for everyone to come in?" frowned Aaryan.

To which Mr Sehgal replied definitively, "We are all here. Let's begin!"

Aaryan registered a lot of speculative glances coming his way and cursed his lack of focus when it came to Gayatri.

I should be grateful that she is not here anymore, else I would have probably given away the entire company to these guys. She continues to bewitch me. Need to stay miles away from her, with the firm resolution in his head, AK spent the next three hours overlooking the proceedings and only intervening when required.

At tea break, he walked up to Prateek and Vinod and grudgingly admitted that they had come up with some great suggestions.

"How can I have a flat tyre at this hour!" wailed Gayatri as she stood next to her car in the parking lot.

Sushant walked up and teased, "Why don't you degrade the car's rating for its below average performance?"

Seeing her belligerent expression, he backed off and offered to change her tire. Sheepishly, she informed him that the spare was also in the same state. Blushing a little, he offered her a ride on his bike.

To which she said, "No, you have a long way to go, and that too, in the opposite direction."

Gayatri called the mechanic from a nearby garage and decided to wrap up some more work till then.

"But you told me it shall be done and the mechanic would come and put the tyres back. What do you mean there is no one at the workshop anymore? How can the man leave without finishing my job or at least informing me about it?"

Frustrated to the core, she disconnected the call midway.

"What is the problem?" asked the deep voice belonging to her very own Greek God.

Reluctantly turning around to face him, she realised that they were not alone. In fact, it seemed that the meeting had finished just now and everyone including Taruna and Vikram had come down together.

Taruna linked her arms through Gayatri's and said impishly, "You look miserable. We are all going for dinner at the much touted Kebab Factory after a gruelling day. Why don't you join us? You don't mind right, AK?"

Gayatri squeezed Taruna's arm and said, "Another day, I promise. It's been a long day."

"Why don't you go ahead and join the others. I'll join in a bit," he said firmly.

Looking from one to the other, Taruna smiled her acquiesce and went towards the waiting car.

"Why can't you just tell me what the issue is," he asked irritated as soon as they were alone again.

"You don't need to show fake concern for me. Please carry on with your plan," she replied haughtily.

"Will you tell me or will I have to worm it out of you?" he threatened.

With nostrils flaring, she said, "Oh, I'd like to see you try. Who do you think you are? Playing high and mighty all the time, ordering people around, saying whatever comes to your head."

Fists clenched, breath coming fast and with flushed face, Aaryan thought Gayatri looked glorious.

"You need to calm down first. Maybe I went a bit too far in the morning. But that is your fault. You had goaded me with your new-found loyalty towards Eternity."

Guilt flooded though her due to the grain of truth in his accusations.

"Uh, my car has a flat tyre. Am just calling a cab," she said.

"I'll drop you on the way to the dinner and can we not argue or fight over this, please?" he said, humour finally lacing his words.

"But it is in the opposite direction…" she protested feebly.

Not paying heed to her, Aaryan beckoned his waiting car and opened the door for her. His smell engulfed her and the dark interiors heightened the sense of delicious intimacy.

They reached her residence in what seemed like no time.

"What is wrong with the traffic in this city? Not even one road jam or diversion came on our way to delay the arrival," thought Aaryan savagely.

Gayatri quietly expressed her thanks, before exiting the car.

Watching her walk away, Aaryan was badly tempted to ask her to come back, but refrained from making a total a°° of himself. He had to drag himself mentally to the dinner where everyone had been awaiting his long delayed arrival.

▼

"Did the mechanic reach on time?" asked her mother.

Gayatri steadily looked at her, "Aaryan Kapoor dropped me home. Our company is merging with his and today was the first day I met him. I know I haven't told you all of this earlier, but that's because I didn't want to talk or think about him. To cut a long story short, we are now behaving professionally with each other."

Taken aback at her daughter's abrupt tone, Mrs Vohra knew there was much more to the story than what was being shared.

Neena voiced her concerns to her husband, "She is very vulnerable and still very much attached to that guy than I had believed her to be. I don't know how to help her."

Raj Vohra asked his wife to show some trust in their daughter's capability to manage her life and its challenges.

"Our daughter is much clearer in her head now and has matured in the past year or so. And we are here to support her in any way that she needs."

The next day Gayatri was a mass of nerves. She tried hard to not think about AK's presence in the building. And he materialised right next to her as if she had conjured him up. Hastily, she scrambled to stand up, knocking off the mug kept on her table.

"What are you doing here?" she hissed.

Raising an imperial eyebrow, he beckoned her to turn back and see the whole group. JBCN team was on an official tour of Eternity as the merger had been formally announced in the office that very morning. Looking around, Aaryan had expected to see some bright knick knacks or some sort of memorabilia, but to his surprise, there was absolutely nothing of personal nature in her cabin. Recalling the huge board that she used to have in her cubicle at JBCN with photos of everyone important to her, he wondered about the reason for such austerity here.

"You seem to be doing well for yourself here. Mr Malhotra has only the best things to say about your professionalism and knowledge," praised a proud Sudhir to her.

"The credit goes completely to you, Sudhir. I learnt a lot from you during my stint at JBCN. You were a great boss," she replied emotionally.

Aaryan was the last one to leave the room, with a cryptic parting shot, "You have changed!" which kept her pondering over it all through the evening, much to her irritation.

She reached the hotel that evening to meet Taruna.

"I forgot to ask for her room number," she smiled at Vikram whom she bumped into at the hotel steps.

Vikram took her up with him to his room and called up Taruna to join them in there.

"Finally I get to see you. And what is this polite expression that you wear all the time these days? You have been acting all formal in the office also. Where is the famous laughter fountain of yours?" he rattled off.

Within fifteen minutes, Gayatri had been transported back to her old self, helplessly laughing over Vikram's antics and Taruna's mimicry.

"By the way, who is that weird guy who is claiming to marry you soon?" asked Vikram.

Water spluttered in Gayatri's mouth upon hearing this as the bell chimed.

Sudhir along with AK entered the room.

"We seem to have come at the wrong time," said Sudhir as a stone faced Aaryan looked at Gayatri in her casual tee and skinny pants with her trademark braid.

This was the first time he was catching a glimpse of the girl he knew a couple of years ago. With blush enhancing her make-up free face, he thought her to be the prettiest creature alive on earth.

"No no, please come in," said Vikram jovially.

"This was a girls' evening out which I have gate crashed and we would be happy if you both joined in as well," he invited them in.

Sudhir hesitated before saying, "We were going down to grab some dinner and thought of asking you to come along."

Taruna came to the door and said, "We have ordered food enough for a twenty people party. So please help us in finishing it."

Shrugging, AK walked into the room with Sudhir following suit.

"So coming back to the question, who is the guy?" asked Vikram, looking at Gayatri.

Nonplussed, she looked at him with a blank expression.

Before Vikram could muddle it any further, Taruna intervened, "The second evening after being thrashed by team Eternity, I was standing at the water cooler in the coffee room when I overheard a couple of guys. One of them talked about you being wonderful and that he planned to propose to you right after the negotiations got over."

Acutely aware of AK's interested gaze, Gayatri tried to play it down, "He is a pest and nothing more. I have tried to tell him off numerous times, but to no avail. So now I simply ignore him."

Thankfully for her, the food arrived by then.

"This is so much fun, reminds me of the time when we used to have food marathons in the cafeteria with Gayatri treating us as her guinea pigs," chortled Vikram.

An indignant Gayatri responded tartly, "I think your memory is failing you. My dishes were extremely famous and much appreciated by everyone, especially you, who came up with new demands almost every day."

As Sudhir joined in with his anecdotes as well, it was a noisy affair which had everyone enjoying the meal and camaraderie between old friends.

Gayatri got up to wash her hands, followed by Aaryan.

"So how is the lover boy? Still in Singapore or is he back in India?" he asked, standing at the threshold of the washroom.

Stumped by his timing and the question, Gayatri struggled to come up with a neutral response, "He is doing very well and yes, he is permanently settled in Singapore now."

While his heart took a beating at the news, he persisted, "Which means you shall also be joining him sooner than later, and we'll lose a valuable asset in the company."

She responded haughtily, "I don't see how that is of any concern to you. I report to Mr Sehgal and any plans of mine which affect the company shall be conveyed to him."

Closing the space between them, he spoke softly, "But you see you are forgetting something vital. I own Mr Sehgal and his company lock stock and barrel now. So any allegiance that you have to him automatically gets transferred to me."

Gayatri walked past him wordlessly. She told everyone that it was time she left and would see them at work the next day.

"I should have known. He would never change. Always ready with his venomous arrows, I just hate him…" she swore.

Her arm was yanked from behind at the elevator door and she came face-to-face with the villain of the moment.

"Why did you leave without answering my question? And why are you crying?" said Aaryan, noticing her teary eyes.

"What do you care whether I cry or laugh? Just leave me alone," she said miserably.

The elevator door opened and AK walked into it, taking Gayatri with him.

Pressing the stop button, he tipped up Gayatri's stricken face and asked again, "Why are you crying? Is it because of something I said or did?"

Concern marred his face as Gayatri looked up at him, "You have just no idea, do you? It's nothing, I am just tired. It has been a long stressful week and I just want to go home now..."

And rest of her sentence went into his mouth. He finally plunged into doing what his heart had been waiting for since he had seen her. After the initial resistance, her treacherous body gave up the battle. Holding her as if she was made out of gossamer silk, Aaryan left her mouth to leave a trail of feverish kisses all across her face; eyes closed and lips swollen, she looked like a sensuous goddess out to wreck the senses of the mortals and he simply couldn't get enough of her.

Her pulse fluttered wildly at the base of her neck and Aaryan swooped down to suckle it. He was turning her crazy with his actions and she couldn't stop herself from luxuriating in his arms.

"You drive me mad, always have," he murmured into her ear, as his teeth nipped lightly on her earlobe.

The elevator dinged, announcing their arrival on the sixteenth floor. Realising that he was no longer pushing the stop button, AK shielded a dazed Gayatri from the curious looks of the couple entering the lift. He caught her by the arm and got out.

"Where are we going?" she asked, finally getting a bearing of her surroundings.

Without answering her, he opened his room and propelled her inside.

Panic setting in, Gayatri tried to lunge for the door handle, but AK caught her and held her close, "Shush... it's okay. We just need you to start breathing again before I let you leave, lest you faint halfway home."

"This is crazy. How can we be fighting one minute and then…"

Gayatri couldn't complete her sentence as she took in AK's intense expression.

Drawing her into his arms, he whispered, "Would you be able to handle the truth?"

At her mute expressions, he continued in his hypnotic voice, "Our bodies have a strong affinity for each other for some unfathomable reason; and that attraction is so strong that it drowns out all possible dislike or aversion that we may feel for one another."

Unable to utter any words, she simply shook her head and tried stepping out of his embrace, but he immediately tightened his arms around her, "Tell me now…"

At her befuddled expressions, he clarified, "I am referring to your reason for crying upon my asking you about that Singapore guy."

Spurred into action by his statements, Gayatri shoved him aside and mocked him, "You want to know the truth behind my reaction? First tell me why does it matter to you that I am upset or happy? You had ruthlessly judged me last year and found me lacking. How does my future or past interest you?"

With no reply forthcoming, she carried on her tirade, "What about all the names you called me that day? Why? Who gave you that right? And more importantly, on what basis did you form such an opinion about me?"

"It doesn't affect me anymore, but you had hurt me deeply then. I was at a very low point of my life and you had increased my misery with your venomous words," saying so, she opened the door and left a shocked AK staring at her retreating back.

Within a few moments of Gayatri's leaving, there was a knock and Aaryan ran to open the door, only to find a grim looking Sudhir. Disappointed, he invited Sudhir inside, shutting the door.

"Under normal circumstances, I would have never intervened or shared what I am about to, right now," he started.

His mind still not out of the conversation with Gayatri, AK took a little while to comprehend Sudhir's words, "On my way to your suite, I saw Gayatri at the elevator."

"I am not here to lecture or admonish you, but to share what little I know and hope that helps clear the air out between you two," said Sudhir.

"After her quitting, her office mails had been forwarded to my account, as per the standard practice to maintain continuity. Unintentionally, I stumbled upon one of her personal mails. It was from a lady named Rachna and she was apparently a friend of Gayatri's. The gist of the mail, as per my understanding, was that Gayatri had taken a trip to Singapore to test the truth of her relation with her boyfriend, since she was confused because of her strong feelings for her boss here. I assume that she was not referring to me," said Sudhir wryly.

He continued, "Because I clearly remember not having the remotest romantic interlude with her, which the mail alludes to. Coming back to the point, the lady repeatedly kept apologising for her blunder due to which Gayatri and umm… Nakul were no longer together."

Aaryan berated him for not coming forward with this piece of news earlier.

"One, I was not privy to what transpired between the two of you, and second, by the time I read this mail, she had already left town and you seemed to have been unaffected by it," said Sudhir defensively.

He continued, "I would have not raked up this issue even now, had it not been for the very visible tension between the two of you."

After his HR head left, AK decided to not jump to any conclusions, instead to try and find out for the first time what had actually transpired all those months ago. The next morning marked the scheduled arrival of JBCN's lawyers and AK got caught up in the legalities involved in the merger agreement signing.

Gayatri didn't see or hear from AK after that for the next five days, "That is how he has always been, self-centred, bordering on being cruel."

The merger was officially signed on Friday and in order not to lose the brand value, the merged company was going to be referred to as JBCN Corp.

"I am back to square one, again an employee of JBCN," thought Gayatri morosely as her mailbox pinged the arrival of a new mail.

Apparently the entire organization had been invited for a celebration at one of latest lounges in south Delhi that same night.

At lunch time, Taruna dropped in to catch up with Gayatri. "Can you pick me up for the party tonight? I don't want to tag along the boys."

Hesitating, Gayatri confessed, "But I am not sure if I'll make it to the celebrations tonight."

"Whattt? You are Eternity's shining star and now onwards you officially belong to us. So unless you want me to bring in the higher powers to force you, you better come of your own accord."

Left with no choice, Gayatri complied and agreed to see Taruna at the hotel gate at 8 p.m.

Debating what to wear, Gayatri discarded six dresses before settling on a demure cream coloured, knee length dress. Replacing her solitaire earrings for a pair of long gold danglers, she wore her favourite mute gold, high heeled sandals.

"You are going to knock the socks off the Delhi guys," said a delighted Gayatri at the vision that Taruna presented.

Clad in a red off-shoulder top, she looked stunning.

"Thank you for boosting my ego, but what happened to you? Did all the colours vanish from your wardrobe? You look more suited for a Darby luncheon than a rocking night out," commented Taruna.

Shrugging, Gayatri replied, "That is the look I prefer these days."

Sick of the business talk all around him, Aaryan was ready to scream in frustration. He hadn't been able to catch even a reflection of Gayatri in the past few days, forget talking to her, and Sudhir's words were driving him crazy. The only thing that he had understood was that Gayatri had felt strongly enough for him, to jeopardize her long standing relation with Nakul at that time. Oscillating between hope and despair, he decided that if she did not turn up in the next half hour, he would go over to her house.

Lost in his thoughts, he suddenly became aware of someone shouting on the mike, "You Dilliwallahs obviously don't know how to party. So we are going to show you the right way of having a swell time," shouted Taruna.

Aaryan shook his head at his people's antics as he watched someone trying to drag her off the dance floor.

"She has finally arrived!" his heart recognised the lustrous hair and the luminous skin of his, oh yes, his HR!

Physically restraining himself from going ahead and hugging her, he laughed out loud at the tableau in front of him. While Vikram and Taruna were being mobbed by the absolutely indignant ex-Eternity employees, Gayatri valiantly tried to act as the peacemaker between the two parties.

"The ruckus needs to be stopped before there is any bloodbath on that floor," said Vinod dryly to AK.

"You move out of my way, Gayatri. These two pansies challenged Delhi's warm blooded species and they will be given a befitting answer," said an overly passionate Rahul Chaddha.

"Please control your emotions, she was obviously jesting," said a harrowed Gayatri as she dragged Taruna off the podium.

"I am not going to let you take her away before I show her our capabilities," said Rahul as he held Gayatri's free arm, using the opportunity to try and cosy up to her.

"Unhand her right now and henceforth let me not catch you within a two hundred metre radius of her ever again, else you'll be really sorry," said Aaryan, looking ready to murder the man.

Vikram intervened and took a shaken looking Rahul away from there.

"I apologise AK, didn't realise it would get so out of hand," said Taruna contritely.

Focussing on Gayatri, he asked savagely, "And what about you? Do you have to go and save the entire world? Just jumped in without thinking twice."

"If you are done with your lecture quota for the day, I would like to go and meet some of my colleagues," she said frostily.

Suddenly contrite, Aaryan decided to let his real emotions surface, "You can chat later. It's been really long since I danced with someone who knows her moves," and gave her a twirl on the floor.

Surprise flitted across her face at the complete changeover in his mood. Aaryan felt ecstatic and kept her pressed close to him for the entire duration of the three or four songs (he had lost count!)

"Shit, I am crazy about her!" he thought to himself as they drew apart because the DJ announced that dinner was served and they came back to their senses.

"Who ordered dinner?" muttered AK to himself while Gayatri nearly ran out of the place, without uttering a single word to him.

Dabbing her inflamed face with cold water in the washroom, she stared at her image, disgusted at the absolute collapse of her self-control around that *man*.

"What is wrong with me? How can I forget his behaviour with me over these past few days?" she thought wretchedly.

She made up her mind to not return to the party. But the minute she opened the door of the washroom, her head crashed into none other than Aaryan's chest.

"What are you doing loitering around women's loo?" she demanded indignantly.

"You were taking so long inside that I had begun to wonder if all was fine. I had almost decided to take a peek inside myself," he said innocently.

All Gayatri could do was stare at the man. Never been exposed to the charming side of AK, she couldn't handle the unexpected mischief that lurked in his eyes, especially after the recent intimacy on the dance floor.

He brought his hand to her cheek and spoke huskily, "You seem warm. Can I get you anything, a soda or a glass of wine?"

Mutely shaking her head, Gayatri flushed even further when Aaryan took her hand and started proceeding towards the party hall.

"What are you doing? First dancing with me on the floor like that and now publicly holding my hand?" yelped Gayatri.

"Why should there be a reason for everything? Can we not do something just because it gives us pleasure?" he asked gently.

"I want to go home, I am feeling a bit tired," said Gayatri.

Fighting for more time with her, he told her that she needed to grab a bite before he could let her go back home.

"But I am not hungry at all," she protested.

Aaryan didn't listen to her gripe and took her towards the table where the food had been laid. Almost everyone was still in the lounge area, so they found themselves a corner table.

Unable to take his eyes off her face, Aaryan wanted the moment to go on forever, but the next minute, his neck was ensnared by a pair of long arms.

"Hi darling, long time no see," pouted a scantily clad woman.

Groaning inwardly, AK pasted a fake smile on his face. Not daring to meet Gayatri's eyes, AK sent the lady packing as soon as he could without being outright rude. Gayatri thought her body colour would turn green with the amount of jealousy she was experiencing.

He always surrounds himself with anorexic women. God knows why he is showing interest in me. I am far far away from size zero, she thought enviously.

But before she could react, he sat with one knee bent on the floor.

"Please don't be angry with me. That pesky woman means absolutely nothing to me," he said.

She feared that she would turn into a puddle right there and then.

She lied outright, "Why should I get upset if you are catching up with a good friend of yours. Anyway, I really want to get going."

He got up reluctantly and called up his driver.

A surprised Gayatri gaped at him and said, "Surely you are not planning on dropping me home?"

Grimacing, AK replied, "Why does that surprise you so much? Don't you know me even a little by now? But unfortunately, I can't leave from here tonight, so my driver shall follow you and safely see you home and then return."

Gayatri started to giggle, "You do know that I do this all the time. There is absolutely no need for a chaperone."

He closed whatever miniscule gap was between them and replied huskily, "I don't care about the time that I am not around, but when I am, it is my responsibility to see to your err, well-being, so don't argue with me."

I am falling for him so hard all over again that this time there would be no coming back, thought Gayatri panicking at the close proximity.

Aaryan insisted on dropping her till the hotel porch and barely restrained himself from caressing her one last time before he let her go. Smiling like a loony, he walked back into the hotel.

▼

Joining work on Monday, Gayatri was a little disappointed and confused about AK's change of behaviour and her own reactions. To top it, after the newfound peace, she had secretly hoped for some sort of communication over the weekend, but sadly, the mailbox and phone remained bereft of anything from him. The day also didn't look very promising because the pink slips were being prepared by her team for the marked employees.

"AK left early morning on Saturday itself, and we'll also leave tonight. Rest of the stuff can be done over mails or teleconferences," Taruna told Gayatri later that morning.

"I should go meet Sudhir once before he leaves then," said Gayatri, trying to hide her acute disappointment over the news.

Walking towards the conference room, Gayatri muttered to self, "I should have known he'll behave in such a fashion. I should have realised that when I saw that woman on Friday night, draping herself all over him. Stupid stupid girl... how many times do you need to be rejected by the same guy before you learn your lesson?"

▼

"How long will it take before the results are known, Doc?" asked a frantic Aaryan. He had received a hysterical call from his mother on Saturday early morning telling him that his father had vomited blood and was struggling to breathe that very moment. The doctors had run a battery of tests post the initial check-up, while both mother and son had kept a vigil outside Rohit Kapoor's ICU room.

"We should have the prognosis within the hour," assured Dr Bandhopadhya to AK.

"I should have paid more attention to his health," wailed his mother.

Comforting her, Aaryan refused to think beyond the test results, though their main business and legal advisor was on his way to the hospital.

"There is a tumour in Mr Kapoor's stomach and the problem is that the endoscopy is currently inconclusive in terms of its malignancy because of where it is located. But as of now, we need to operate and remove it urgently," said the doctor plainly.

Mr Walia, the lawyer, clapped AK on his shoulder and took him to the cafeteria.

"This is not life-threatening yet. We can hold off the press and public for a while before we get a clearer picture," said Mr Walia soothingly.

"Do what you have to, keep the vultures away. Apart from you, the doctor, mom and me, no one else knows the details and we want to keep it that way till the operation is done," said Aaryan ruthlessly.

"Don't worry, your father and I have been together for more than forty years. You can trust me," assured Mr Walia.

"May I suggest a plan to you which will serve our dual purpose of getting the best possible treatment for Rohit and to shield us from the unwanted media attention? Let's use the PR department to publicize a family vacation for the three of you to America. We will release some old family holiday pictures to authenticate the same. Just leave the details to me. You concentrate on your father's well-being," he said.

Refusing to succumb to the gravity of the situation, Aaryan concentrated on organising every small little detail, from the doctor's appointment in the US to the departure time from India. Anjali Kapoor, who had been a pillar of strength for the Kapoor men all throughout, suddenly looked fragile and was leaning heavily on her son for emotional support. With all the arrangements completed, they flew out Sunday night.

▼

It had been two weeks since the merger and things were working better than before due to a seamless synergy between the two companies. Gayatri was enjoying her work and had been awarded with more responsibilities. The only blip was the whole weekend romance, which now seemed like a dream gone bad and she was trying her best to get over it and move on. The final nail in the coffin had been that page 3 news about AK and his family vacationing in America along with his new arm candy, some Brazilian model. After crucifying herself for being so gullible again, she vowed to never ever speak to the man, even if it meant leaving the company.

▼

The nerve-wracking experience was finally over, or so Aaryan hoped. The endless wait at the New York hospital, while his father was undergoing surgery, had been killing, not to mention the fast deteriorating condition of his mother.

"I am extremely pleased to inform you that the tumour that we removed from your father's intestines is not cancerous," said Dr Saint Claire.

Mother-son duo sagged against each other in acute relief. Aaryan had stayed with his father for a week.

"This is simply too much pressure for Dad, at this age. He cannot be allowed to continue like this, we'll have to come up with the alternate plan soon enough," AK had argued with his father and the lawyer.

"I fully agree with you, AK, and I think it is time that we rolled out the succession plan that your father had charted out a few years ago," said Mr Walia.

He continued, "The time has come sooner than we anticipated, but we have always been prepared. You have to understand that this is a time consuming process laden with lots of approvals and boring board meetings, but you need to step up to the task."

Rohit Kapoor took up, where his lawyer had left, "I shall soon be moving to the role of Chairman Emeritus, which is a non-executive role, but I shall only do this post we manage to pass the resolution in the parent company about you taking over as MD within the next one year. You have been on the boards of all our companies for a long time now. But going forward, we need to change your inactive status to an operating one. You will need to start playing a much aggressive role in your legacy."

'Billionaire heir finally grows up to fill Daddy's shoes,' screamed the newspaper headlines.

There had been ongoing rumours about a new CEO to join in, but now it seemed they had held more than a grain of truth in them. Going forward, AK would only be present in the non-executive head role. So much for her giving cold shoulder to him when he came to the Delhi office next time, thought Gayatri ruefully. In the light of this news, she wasn't sure if she'd ever see him again.

"Please ensure that all loose ends have been tied and there is no unforeseen complication that we have left to chance," instructed an impatient AK to his team of executive assistants. He had moved to his father's office and had inherited Sr. Kapoor's competent line-up of staff.

"What is so urgent that you need to fly down to Delhi in the middle of things, AK?" asked Mr Walia, who was a regular feature at Aaryan's office these days.

"It's something personal and I have delayed it long enough," said Aaryan, thinking of the past one month of hectic lobbying and wetting his feet in the untested waters. Though Gayatri hadn't been away from his mind, there had been simply too much on his plate for him to go see her and talk things out. As long as she was still with JBCN, he knew all was okay, and though she may be mad at him currently, he was confident that she would come around eventually. One of the nights last week, post ungodly working hours, he had been sleepless and had searched the Facebook on an impulse for a glimpse of Gayatri. And what a revelation that had been! Not only did he find her beautiful pictures, but also the recent posts about Nakul getting married, (thankfully) to someone else.

"It is wonderful to see you here, AK. Many congratulations on the new role," said Vinod on Friday evening as Aaryan landed in the JBCN office.

Acknowledging him and the others as they offered felicitations, Aaryan looked around for Gayatri in vain. All employees, manager level and above, had been asked to come up to the corporate floor. Eventually he asked Vinod for her whereabouts.

"Well, she had a pre-approved day off today," he said a touch defensively.

Assuring him that it as just a polite enquiry, Aaryan didn't want to wait till the next day and called her up on her cell. But after four unanswered calls, he gave up.

AK (His Royal Highness!) has decided to bestow me with not one but four calls. And he naturally assumes that I shall bend backwards to pick up the phone. Whatever sarcastic barbs he wants to send my way can wait till tomorrow, thought Gayatri, desperately retraining her hands lest they pick up the call out of their own accord.

"Do they still serve the best Bulls-Eye at Machan?" asked Dev, Gayatri's cousin after dinner. He was referring to the signature dessert dish at the coffee shop at Taj Mansingh Hotel in South Delhi.

Laughing, Gayatri told him that the dessert was still the best there.

"So let's go there now," he begged.

"Now? It is eleven in the night and it's a good thirty minute drive even at this hour. Remember you have an early morning flight back?" asked a surprised Gayatri.

"I am game, if you are," he cajoled.

"I think I will call it a night. It is almost 4 a.m. in Australia right now," said the sleepy looking client to AK.

They were out for drinks at the famous lounge bar at Taj Mansingh.

"Sure, whatever you say Nick; though you should grab a quick bite with all those cocktails swimming in you right now. The coffee shop is right next door and serves some good authentic Indian fare," suggested Aaryan.

With no call back or even a monosyllabic message from Gayatri, he was feeling depressed and didn't relish the prospect of a long lonely night ahead before 'hopefully' seeing her the next day.

"I swear I shall take my revenge a hundred times over from her for torturing me like this," he thought to himself.

As they waited to be seated by the maitre d'hotel, Aaryan saw a familiar looking profile partially hidden by the elevated podium. With his pulse rate leaping, AK didn't leave it to chance and with a quick apology to Nick, moved towards the table where Gayatri sat with a stranger.

"I can't imagine someone who has lived in Paris for more than six years, is mad about dessert in India. I mean France is heaven for someone who has a sweet tooth," exclaimed Gayatri.

With his mouth full, he responded with a wink, "You won't understand. There are a thousand memories with this bulls-eye – countless night outs and dates."

Laughing, Gayatri was suddenly aware of a presence next to her.

"And here I thought you were in some dire condition, hence not picking up repeated calls from your boss," said Aaryan through clenched teeth, absolutely unhappy to see her with some new guy.

What is with her and men? Got one hanging around all the time, AK thought savagely.

Flustered to see AK in flesh, Gayatri fumbled before answering, "All is well, thank you for your concern, *Boss*. For your information, I am on approved leave though."

Without acknowledging her caustic answer, he extended his hand to the man next to her, "Hi, Aaryan Kapoor."

Shaking his hand vigorously, Dev introduced himself and said, "Of course, I know you along with most of the people remotely associated with the financial sector, worldwide."

Nodding, he turned to her and said, "I need to speak with you urgently."

She felt like slapping him and screaming, "You are more than a month late in wanting a conversation with me."

Sedately she replied, "I'll be at my desk 9 a.m. sharp. Right now, I think your friend is looking for you."

Belatedly realising that he had completely forgotten about Nick, Aaryan bid a polite bye to Dev before giving her an intense look.

In long strides, he went up to Nick and apologised for deserting him for so long and pointed the table with a clear view to Gayatri's to the hovering waiter, "We'll take that table."

"Be careful, that mug probably can't handle your mercurial temperature right now," said Nick wryly.

Watching Gayatri laughing with that guy, Aaryan's anger was threatening to attain new heights.

How dare she? What the hell is wrong with her? Is one guy not good enough for her? Can she not figure out that I am mad about her…I fu******* love her, he finally admitted to himself.

Operating on zero sleep and half a bottle of Lagavulin, AK resembled a surly bear when Gayatri saw him perched at her desk at 9.30.

"You are late, Ms Vohra," he addressed her in his deep voice, roughened by the lack of sleep.

"How can he look and sound so damn sexy first thing in the morning," she thought crossly, as Sushant and Veer looked at her expectantly for an answer.

Deliberately goading him, she replied sweetly, "I had a really late night, Mr Kapoor, but I promise to stay back half hour extra at work today."

Looking at her smug expressions, he barked at the two assistants to take a break while he discussed some important matters with their boss.

"What is your problem? What must be going through their heads right now?" said an irritated Gayatri.

"Honestly, I don't care about what they think is happening in this room, but if you want to do this in front of them, I can call them back," he challenged with a raised eyebrow.

"And what exactly are we doing in this room?" she retorted.

Giving her an intense look, he replied smoothly, "There are a lot of things that I can think of doing here, but for now, let's restrict ourselves to a frank conversation, starting with your latest puppy."

Blushing deeply, Gayatri brazened it out by going on the offensive, "You flatter yourself and underestimate me. As for your query, my personal life is not and has never been a matter of concern to you. So if there is nothing else that you have to say to me, I suggest you leave."

Aaryan started walking towards her till she was backed up against the wall. Putting his hands on the wall, he effectively imprisoned her before whispering silkily, "Never throw a challenge that you are not ready to follow through."

He stared into her liquid eyes, "I don't want any more games between us now. And your personal life became my concern since you started invading mine. So I have all the right in the world."

His high handed attitude finally got to Gayatri.

She lashed out at him, "Who do you think you are – God? Today you are in a benevolent mood, so you'll speak to me nicely but you are not answerable to me for all the previous times when you treated me like dirt. The moral compass with which you measure other people doesn't apply to you. Why is that? And why should I tell you who was I with? Have I ever questioned you when I see women drape themselves all over you?"

Livid with him now, she didn't give him a chance to reply and continued ranting, "You spend two days flirting with me and then suddenly you get bored and decide to entertain yourself elsewhere. And then you come back again when the mood strikes, expecting me to be ready and waiting to fall in your lap… guess what? *I am not interested.* My parents are looking for a suitable groom for me and it is with my consent."

Taking in the shocked expression on AK's face, Gayatri felt a sense of elation at her white lie.

"Foolish girl, what were you hoping for – a declaration of love and proposal to marry you?" thought a deflated Gayatri when he walked out of the cabin without saying another word.

AK did not know when or how he got back to Mumbai. Her words were still ringing in his ears – her reproach and her hurt evident in every nuance of her body.

Out of ideas, he turned to his mother for her help.

"You men can be so blind! How could you not see her affection for you all this while? And how could you have doubted her integrity after working in such close quarters with her? I always did wonder about her abrupt leave from JBCN back then, but I have always tried not to interfere in your personal life. Now I wish I had. Let me tell you something upfront, If I were in her place, I would've probably slapped you and would have never wanted to see your face ever again. You not only withdrew your affection, but were downright mean to her when she probably needed you the most, and all because of your preconceived notions," said Mrs Kapoor, scathingly.

"Mom, you are not aiding me right now by giving what is probably the worst dressing down of my life," said AK, self-pityingly.

Continuing her tirade, Mrs Kapoor retorted, "Really, even at this moment, you expect me to mollycoddle you?"

Aaryan hugged his mother and told her, "I need you to help me right now, Mom. You are welcome to scold me for the rest of your life… just don't do it at this moment."

Anjali mellowed down but couldn't resist a parting shot, "What kind of help are you looking for – to forget her and move on, or to find a way to get you back in her life?'

Exasperated, he said, "You are not going to let me off the hook so easily, are you? Of course I want her to be with me. I admit that I have been blindly arrogant and conceited. But I swear to you, I am going to make up for all that, if she gives me a chance."

Ever since her showdown with AK, all the colours had gone away from Gayatri's life. It felt like her life had been rewound and she was back to sticking glue to the various broken pieces of her heart. It was becoming difficult to even put up a facade in front of everyone around.

She sent a mail to Vinod requesting for a week off from work.

"How can you even think of taking a leave right now? Don't forget that we are still in the hundred-day integration plan zone and there is enough work on everyone's plate, including yours," he admonished.

Mr Sehgal walked in as Gayatri got up to leave from her boss's cabin.

"Good that I found you both here," he said.

At their enquiring looks, he grinned and said, "You both look so worried and you should because I have got more work for you."

Their collective groans vibrated in the room.

Mr Sehgal said laughingly, "Well I treat you all like my family and if one of the family members gets married, there is extra work for everyone else, right?"

He continued to explain, "My daughter Sanjana has decided to get married to her long standing beau, Karan. He is Mr Thapar's son," referring to one of the big steel magnates in Delhi.

The wedding has been fixed for the next month and the weeklong functions shall commence from the 12th of July.

"Many congratulations, sir! It's going to be a monsoon wedding," exclaimed Gayatri, distracted for the moment.

She loved weddings – the varied rituals and the general excitement along with them.

"So I am going to be counting on you to make sure the office is running smoothly and ensuring full participation from the entire organization during the wedding. In any case, after more than 70% layoffs, the people who have been retained are our best people. So let's make sure they feel included. Also, please compile a list for me after coordinating with the Mumbai office about the number and names of the people who need to be invited from there," finished Mr Sehgal.

Vinod said, "Well, that is the answer to your request for leave."

▼

"Hello stranger, do you actually live here or are you just visiting?" asked Raj Vohra to a reticent Gayatri as she sat down for a late dinner.

"Sorry Dad, you know the workload has been immense and hence the working hours are also crazy right now. It is a matter of a couple of weeks more before all merger related formalities as well as my CEO's daughter's wedding would be over. Life shall be back to normal for me then," she explained.

"Are you sure it will be normal, sweetheart?" asked her mother.

"You know I haven't seen my daughter in this house for the past three years now. You left her behind somewhere in Mumbai and haven't even gone back to retrieve her ever."

Surprised at the turn of topic, Gayatri spluttered, "What are you trying to say, Mom?"

She shook her head sadly, "Till now it's only been your father and me who have moved on, but you are still caught up in that nightmare."

"I know that you had a bad experience and the men around you at that time didn't show faith in you, but that does not mean that you destroy yourself for it. The choice has always been in your hand – forgive or fight. In Nakul's case, I would agree that you moved on, but as far as AK is concerned, you are still standing in the martyr's position where you were almost two years back," challenged her mother.

Gayati defended hotly, "You are wrong about it, Mom. I had forgotten all about AK till he came back into my life."

Choosing to stay quiet while the women wrestled it out, Raj looked on in concern, as his wife pushed their daughter harder to get her out of the shell that she seemed to have created around herself for some time now.

"Really? Then where is the twinkle in your eyes, what about the beautiful laughter? Where did all the happiness evaporate from your life and you turned yourself into a pale version of yourself? It was just a romance gone bad, correct? So why did you make a big deal out of it?" questioned her mother passionately.

Furious at her mother for being so insensitive, Gayatri lashed out instinctively, "Romance gone bad? Is that what you think it was for me? I left my bleeding stupid heart there… for the first time in my life I had fallen truly in love."

"But why did you leave, Gayatri? Why did you not stay back and fight for your love? Did you not have faith in yourself?" said her mother gently.

She said hoarsely, "I can't do this anymore. There are things that you have no idea about. I simply hate him now and do not want to ever talk to or about Aaryan Kapoor."

Neena watched her daughter walk out of the living room, pain etched on her face.

The wedding was supposed to take place at the Taj Palace hotel and there was a line-up of interesting theme-based functions through the week.

"I am reaching tomorrow afternoon and would be staying for the next three nights," Taruna said excitedly on the phone to Gayatri.

'Tell me you have your wardrobe figured out for the functions. I simply do not want to see you in drab clothes like you were sporting last time I was in town," warned Taruna.

Challenging Taruna that she would outshine her, Gayatri put down the phone and recalled her reaction in the aftermath of the conversation at her home two weeks ago.

In the wee hours of the morning, her mother had come to her room and quietly sat down next to her, taking Gayatri's head in her lap.

"I never meant to upset you like this, but your father and I have seen you going into a shell slowly for some time now and it was only getting worse," she had said apologetically.

After a reality check, she had realised that most of the things that her mother had pointed out were spot on and Gayatri had a fresh surge of guilt for being so absorbed in her own misery that she had been oblivious to the anguish she had caused her parents all this while.

Vowing to genuinely start afresh, she thought, "I am going to have a great time at the wedding with my friends and going to firmly ignore the unwanted elements who might pop up there."

Though she tried to deny it vehemently, her fervent wish was to knock the socks off that arrogant scoundrel.

"But won't it look rude that we being underlings in the company are walking in so late," Taruna argued.

"We are so junior on the totem pole, that it wouldn't matter when and whether we attend the function. Also, unlike

Mumbaiites who are the punctual ones, it is considered bad manners to walk in early for a Delhi event. It looks like you have nothing better to do with your time," Gayatri laughed into the phone.

Neena Vohra came into the room as Gayatri finished her call and twirled to show her outfit to her mother. Clad in a voluminous sea green lehenga with a backless light pink choli, Gayatri showed off her hourglass figure to perfection. With a dozen bangles jingling on both the arms, her eyes were adorned with kohl while she kept the lips nude. The braided hair was bejewelled with a maang teeka and chaand ballis adding sparkle to her face. The only thing that she had been hesitating before her mother came in, was a diamond stud to be worn on her belly button.

"Do you think it'll be too much, Mom? It is an office party, after all," she asked unsurely.

"I personally think it is going to make you look hot," Neena said with a wink.

As soon as Gayatri left home to pick Taruna, Neena called up Anjali Kapoor and told her that her daughter was on her way. Recalling the phone call that Neena had received from Mrs Kapoor almost a month ago, she had been initially angry at Anjali's defence of her son, but after listening to the circumstances surrounding Rohit Kapoor's sudden illness and its consequences, she had told Anjali that she would need some time before she decided what to do about the situation.

"My son loves your girl madly. And I know that he has acted irresponsibly all this while, but you know how slow men can be, whatever age or stage of life they maybe at. All I am asking you to do is find out if Gayatri feels the same for Aaryan beneath all the hurt and misunderstandings," Mrs Kapoor had said.

After a week of sleepless nights, Neena had raised the topic with her daughter and what a conversation it had been! But it had become blindingly clear to both Neena and Raj that Gayatri was still deeply attached to AK. She had approached Anjali the next day and they had talked about how to clear the air between the children. As both discarded the option of a direct confrontation on the topic, the opportunity had presented itself in the form of the upcoming marriage of Mr Sehgal's daughter. And the two mothers had put their clever heads together.

It was 10.30 by the time Taruna and Gayatri entered the ballroom.

"This is my favourite function in any wedding," exclaimed Gayatri.

At her friend's look of enquiry, she elaborated, "The beautiful traditional Punjabi songs, the smell of mehndi, with all the laughing and dancing, make this such a happy event."

"Well, why don't we also get it done? I definitely want a tattoo on my shoulder and maybe one on the forearm," said Taruna impatiently.

Gayatri tried to look around for AK surreptitiously, but to no avail.

"Maybe he will come only for the wedding. After all, he is a very busy man now," she thought irritably.

Finding an empty spot, the ladies sat down to get the mehndi done.

"Let's find ourselves a quiet spot where we can sit and dry our mehndi and probably grab a bite," said Gayatri to Taruna.

The girls settled down to see the dance performances of the various family members. A couple of times, Gayatri felt that prickling at the back of her neck as if she was being observed, but looking around, she found no one. With the humid weather, the henna on her hands was taking long to dry up and Gayatri was extremely thirsty by now. Loathe to spoil the wet design, she hailed a waiter carrying water and picked the sealed bottle, but before she could ask him to unscrew it for her, he walked away to another table. Grimacing, she tried to use her fingertips but couldn't do it.

"I guess I'll stay thirsty a little while longer," she said to Taruna just as a deep voice addressed her, "Please allow me."

Aaryan opened the bottle and bent it towards Gayatri's lips while she stared at him with her mouth open. Clad in a powder blue kurta with black waistcoat and fitted white pantaloons, Gayatri wondered if she had conjured him up from her dreams. He looked no less than a wicked prince.

"If you don't shut your mouth, the water shall drip down to your dress," said Taruna naughtily.

"Would you like me to stop now?" asked Aaryan huskily as Gayatri nearly finished the mini bottle.

Jerking away from him abruptly, a drop spilled from the bottle and trickled down to her neck. Transfixed by the sight, Aaryan traced its journey with his long index finger stopping the drop from disappearing under the neckline.

"Um-hmm, I think I'll go grab a bite and come," said Taruna wisely. Gayatri's insides had turned into mush. She tried hard to find her much needed anger and bitterness against this Greek god.

"Oh good, I found you both here," said Mrs Kapoor smoothly.

Groaning inwardly, Gayatri got up to make a quick escape only to be thwarted by the matriarch, "Aaryan, Mr Sehgal was looking for you."

"I was making good progress and would have handled it on my own, but Mum had to come and interfere," he muttered.

For the past month, he had chafed at being restrained from even calling his girl till 'the right time' as per his mother. Today he had been waiting for her to enter impatiently for some time and now at the first opportunity, he had been sent away.

"So, how have you been Gayatri? It's been really long since we met," started Anjali.

Looking elegant as ever in a grey saree with a string of pearls adorning her neck, she had an innocuous ten minute conversation with Gayatri before seamlessly steering the conversation towards how stressful the past few weeks had been for all of them due to Rohit's illness.

"What happened to Mr Kapoor?" asked a concerned Gayatri.

Recounting their nightmare and its ripple effects on their lives, Anjali pointed out to Gayatri that Aaryan had been caught up in this whole chain of events ever since he left from Delhi after the merger.

"But all those pictures about you all holidaying in New York…" asked a confused Gayatri.

"My dear, that is called throwing media off the scent. We did not want to create any undue panic amongst our investors or employees till we did not have a clear picture ourselves. Which is why Aaryan could not share it with the people dearest to him," she said with a gleam in her eyes.

With an urgency that was beyond her control, she halted Anjali Kapoor mid-sentence, murmuring an incoherent excuse and went in search of AK.

"Oh god, all this while I had been cursing him and he was going through what was probably the worst phase of his life and that night at the coffee shop, I was so rude to him," thought Gayatri as she frantically searched for him.

Her task completed for the evening, Mrs Kapoor went back to join the festivities.

In the middle of an intense discussion with Mr Sehgal's brother, Aaryan saw Gayatri waving frantically at him.

He excused himself immediately, "What is wrong?"

Seizing him by the arm, she scolded him, "Why couldn't you tell me? If not at that time, at least when I had seen you last, you should have made a mention about your father's health. Here I was making all sorts of assumptions and..."

AK's face blazed with unnamed emotions.

"I did not know that you cared as much or that my communication or the lack of thereof, would affect you so," said Aaryan in a husky voice.

"It doesn't matter now, but you should have told me," said Gayatri trying to sound unaffected by his proximity or the words.

She took a step to walk away, only to realise that her mehndi had left an imprint on his kurta.

"I am so sorry," she gave an embarrassed look.

"You can always buy me a new one. But pray tell, why are you always ready to run away from me," he asked taking a step towards her.

"Don't be silly," she scoffed and made the excuse of finding Taruna.

"She is having a good time, surprisingly, with your friend Rahul Chaddha and would not appreciate your ill-timed intrusion. Whereas I, on the other hand, have all the time in the world to keep you suitably engaged till she returns," he countered smoothly.

Gayatri's back hit the wall at one of the shaded alcoves without her realising how she had reached there.

"So how is your friend Nakul doing these days?" he asked casually.

Before she could react, he continued, "And his lovely new bride?"

She was unsure about how and when had he gotten to know about Nakul and Rachna.

She shrugged, "They are both fine; back from their honeymoon."

Suddenly closing all the distance between them, Aaryan stared at her, "When I first met you at Eternity, why didn't you tell me that you guys were not together anymore?"

Heart pounding loudly, she took a leaf from his book and replied tongue-in-cheek, "I didn't know you cared about my love life or the lack thereof."

With a growl, he caught her braid and pulled it sharply, bringing her face in focus, "You have a sassy mouth which I am sorely tempted to shut right now, but considering this is neither the place nor the time for it, I suggest you don't provoke me any further."

Incensed at his high and mighty attitude, Gayati fumed.

Looking at her belligerent expressions, he said, "Let me tell you what all do I care about. Should I start with the thing on your forehead? It makes me want to pull it out with my teeth while I shower kisses all over your face."

Her face flaming, Gayatri unthinkingly put her hand on AK's lips.

"Kindly don't interrupted me. Now the most enticing part… your neck. I am glad it has been left unadorned because I simply love to see that pulse hammering there, just for me. Do you know how many times in the past have I been tempted to leave a mark there, proclaiming you as mine?" he demanded huskily.

"I beg you to stop, please," said Gayatri sagging against the wall.

"Oh, but I haven't reached my favourite part yet. The dilemma is whether to suck the diamond out or embed it further deep inside the navel."

Moaning softly, Gayatri pulled her fingers out of his grasp and hid her fiery face.

"Shall I continue to tell you what else I wish to do with you?" he whispered in her ears.

She pleaded with her eyes to release her from the silken web that he had created around her.

"I shall let you walk away from here on one condition: you will save me a dance and have dinner with me later tonight," he coaxed.

Inordinately shy, she nodded and nearly ran from there.

Before she could regain her equilibrium fully, Taruna grabbed her from behind and scolded her for leaving her alone in the party all by herself.

"Oh really, I heard from a little birdie about some Delhi boy trying to woo you and hence didn't interrupt," said Gayatri.

If Taruna's blush was anything to go by, then the fire wasn't burning on just one side.

"Enough of your smart-ass comments. Now you better show me those Punjabi dance moves," threatened Taruna.

Happy to oblige, Gayatri dived into the overcrowded dance floor with her friend as Aaryan enjoyed his girl's uninhibited dance moves.

"Damn, the one in the green lehenga is too hot man. Check her out," said a voice next to Aaryan.

Realising that the moron next to him was discussing his Gayatri, AK turned around, ready to punch him in the face. Irritated, he walked up to the dance floor and pulled her roughly off the floor.

"What do you think you are doing? How can you be civilised one minute and a brute the very next?" asked an outraged Gayatri.

"My problem is that you are too damn beautiful for your own good. Do you know how many men are staring at you? I want to punch their faces for even lifting their eyes towards you," he admitted savagely.

Speechless when faced with his raw emotions, Gayatri tried to think of an appropriate response when her phone rang. Thankful for a distraction, she picked up her mother's call and moved away. After ten minutes or so, she wrapped up the call, only to find no sign of her sulking boss.

Finding her brooding son, Anjali walked up to him to enquire what was wrong? "Please ask me what is going right? The answer is – nothing. She is always ready to fight with me. I am already going nuts," said Aaryan, frustrated.

"So the cat has finally been belled," said his mother cryptically before giving him an affectionate peck.

"What is with these women in my life? Always demanding answers!" he muttered.

Never ever in her existence had she felt so possessed or wanted as she did today after AK's words. He had literally branded her as his without even a single touch (holding hands didn't count!). It was time to turn the tables; if for nothing else then to give him a taste of his own medicine – all those women whom he paraded in front of her all the time!! She was ravenous and went towards the food section.

"I went to look for you on the dance floor, but instead you are here, breaking your promise to me about eating dinner together," said Aaryan, not willing to stay even few minutes apart from her.

"I wasn't cheating. Just came to scout the options to be better informed when we pick our plates," she said, with a twinkle in her eyes.

They moved from table to table. She was aware of a very different type of intimacy brewing between them, with eyes communicating much more than the innocuous words being exchanged.

"So in the past ten minutes, I have understood that Mexican and Lebanese cuisines rate higher than oriental food in your eyes. And no matter what, your first love would always be anything carnivorous coming out of the tandoor," he teased.

"They make a great pair, Mrs Kapoor," commented Mrs Sehgal when they saw AK and Gayatri make their way to a still empty food hall.

"Considering I haven't seen my son actually pick a plate and eat at a party, that too so early that most of the others haven't even entered the dining area, I would say there is more at play here than empty stomachs," said Anjali with a wink.

"It is late now and I really need to be getting back," said Gayatri a bit reluctantly, after a two-hour stretched meal with more conversation than food morsels. She would have never imagined having a carefree conversation with AK. He had always come across as too intense a person. So it was a pleasant surprise to see him share funny anecdotes with her, keeping the smile perpetually on her face.

"Don't worry about going back. You do know by now that seeing you safely home is one of my favourite tasks," said Aaryan.

Blushing, she said, "Yes, I am aware. But this time help won't be needed. One, Taruna is with me, and secondly, we have my father's driver taking us back home."

"I need you to do two things for me," he told Gayatri expressionlessly.

"I want you to stop calling me AK from now on. My name is Aaryan, and from tomorrow till the wedding is on, my car shall pick you and I'll drop you back every night."

Gayatri asked with a hitch in her throat, "Why not AK? That is what you told me to address you as."

He intertwined his fingers with her henna enriched hand before answering huskily, "Don't you know the answer to the question?"

Her racing heartbeat went on the grand prix route. Murmuring the need to go find Taruna, she bid him good night.

On the way, Gayatri kept wondering about the dichotomy that AK was.

Gayatri tip-toed into the house, not wanting to wake her parents up, but her mother was wide-awake with the latest thriller paperback.

"Hi baby, how was the party?" she asked mischievously, having been updated by AK's mother on the phone already.

She attempted and gave a vague answer before fleeing the room.

Neena Vohra went back to her room, humming and shook her fast asleep husband, "You better start consolidating your savings. I have a feeling we are going to need them soon."

Bewildered at his wife's midnight gibberish, he simply grunted and turned on the other side.

The next day, she was in knee deep work when the phone rang and she responded with her usual, "Good morning, this is Gayatri."

"Yes I know it is you," said a rough, sleep laden sexy voice at the other end.

"Umm... did you need something? I mean...err, why have you called so early and that too on the office line?" she asked, flustered.

Patiently, as if he were addressing a child, he responded, "I needed to hear your voice first thing in the morning after you troubled me and kept me awake the whole night and on the landline because I wanted to surprise you and tell you that I can't wait to see you again."

It was the retro evening and she wanted to dress up especially for AK.....no, Aaryan, she amended hastily in her head and smiled mischievously.

After an hour, she was ready in her 'vintage look' with winged eye liner and red lips. Not wishing to overdo the appearance, she just raised her tresses high and tied a broad glittery black band through them.

The dress that she had chosen for the night was deceptively simple. Black in colour, with a tight fitting bodice, it reached Gayatri's mid thigh. But the highlight was the upper half of the dress which was made out of sheer net, with huge polka dots in black satin all over it. Never exposing, the dress did offer tantalising glimpses of the creamy skin beneath. It had been a pure indulgence on her part on her last trip to London with her parents. A wicked part inside her was urging her to go ahead and bring out her bold and fun side in front of… 'the love of her life'. Yes, she had been in love with him for a long time! But what made it so special now was his reciprocation.

Donning her high heeled black pumps, she was ready and the bell rang right on time. It had been a tad embarrassing explaining to her mother that morning about her reason for not wanting the driver and the car during the next two days. Neena had kept teasing her obliquely till the time Gayatri had made an escape to the office.

"Are you going to propose to her tonight?" Anjali Kapoor dropped the bombshell on her unsuspecting son.

Nearly choking on his glass of wine, AK looked at his mother and warned, "Just because you helped me clear the air, does not mean that you are going to get the inside scoop on my love life."

Anjali laughed and said, "Well, it was worth a try. And anyway, I wanted to know if you needed my help in choosing the right ring or stuff like that."

AK dropped a kiss on his mother's perfumed skin and told her, "Go impress someone else with your stunning Mumtaaz looks. I have things under control now."

Clad in an orange saree with a high bun, Anjali indeed

resembled a famous actress from yesteryears and she was complimented by Gayatri.

"You do know that Aaryan is going to kill you when he sees you looking the way you are," said a delighted Anjali.

She blushed at the reference to her still undefined relation with AK.

"My god, are you hell bent upon giving me a heart attack?" shouted a decidedly not amused AK.

Gayatri gave him an innocent look and told him that if he didn't like what he saw, he could shut his eyes while she went and grooved.

"If you think I am going to let you loose on that floor with lecherous men all around, you must be out of your mind. You want to dance, you do it here and only with me," he announced possessively.

After a few fast songs, the DJ changed the mood and as Diana Ross crooned to 'Endless Love' with Lionel Richie, Aaryan leaned down and wrapped his arms around her, lost in his feelings for this gorgeous woman.

Post the dance, he led her to one of the sofas.

"I have been meaning to share something with you. All that happened in the past arose out of my confused emotions and insecurity. Even when I was angry and hurt about your Singapore trip, I only thought of tormenting you, but would have never let you walk out of my life. But I was too late and you had already gone by then without a word of explanation. All there was left to do was to hold on to my wounded pride," he spoke earnestly.

Unmindful of the people around, she leaned in and hugged him, drawing in his wonderful smell and warmth.

Once Aaryan dropped Gayatri and Taruna back at their respective destinations, he sat back in the car.

"I am crazily, madly in love with this girl. Now the big question is when and how to tell her that?" he wondered aloud, receiving an enquiring look from his bemused driver.

Gayatri took in her feverish expressions in the mirror, flushed cheeks and bright eyes with the frothy toothbrush in her mouth.

Tucked in her bed, Gayatri couldn't wait to see Aaryan the next day.

It was an official holiday for the employees and Gayatri was still lazing around in the house before getting ready for the Rain Dance party.

After a steaming bath, Gayatri, clad in her bathrobe rummaged in the kitchen for something to eat. With a steaming bowl of Maggie, Gayatri settled down with the newspaper in a pair of threadbare shorts with a ratty t-shirt.

About fifteen minutes later, the doorbell rang and frowning Gayatri opened the door. Her jaw dropped at the ten men struggling to stand under the weight of flowers they carried in their hand.

"Are you Gayatri Vohra?" asked one of them panting. Mutely she acknowledged them as they started walking past her into the house, putting the enormous vases filled with the most gorgeous flowers of all varieties. One of them handed over a note to her before filing out. A bemused Gayatri opened the note:

I never got a chance in the past years to ask you about your favourite flower, hence decided to send a few, hoping you will like at least one of them – love always, Aaryan.

"Oh my god, I am so head over heels in love with this guy!" she said aloud, hugging herself before bending down to sniff the tulips, the lilies, the carnations, the amaryllis, the chrysanthemums and some whose names she wasn't sure of!

Grinning, she dialled his number to thank him, but couldn't get through. She thought about how to explain all this to her parents who'd arrive the next morning from a wedding. The bell rang again and she hastened to open the door thinking it was Aaryan. It wasn't him at the door, but a big carton which the man deposited solicitously inside the door. Wondering what the plain container could hold, she hurriedly got a pair of scissors and cut open the bindings. Beautifully bound classics spilled out of the box and Gayatri sat mesmerised looking at what seemed to be complete works of Jane Austen, the Bronte' sisters, Thomas Hardy, Georgette Heyer and many more. The note was attached to her all time favourite *Pride and Prejudice* which read:

I know you must have read most of them, but I wanted to give them to you as they are timeless and one never grows weary of them. Hope you like them – love always, Aaryan

She was charmed beyond measure and couldn't wait to see and confess her overwhelmed emotions to him. The bell rang for the third time, her heart leapt at the possibility of coming face-to-face with him finally. Much to her disappointment, it was his driver with what seemed like bags full of groceries.

"What on earth is he up to now?" she thought in the process of closing the door, only to be stopped by a booted foot.

Aaryan Kapoor, scion to the Kapoor industries and a renowned playboy was holding a similar bag like his driver and asked innocently if he could come in. Reaching up to help him with the bag, Gayatri closed the door behind them and whirled around to stretch and loop her arms through his neck and plant a shy kiss on his lips.

For a second AK went slack with surprise. Recovering quickly, he took over what Gayatri had started and engaged his hands in feeling the damp silken hair, while his mouth explored the crevices and bumps in her mouth. Urging her to open up more, he nipped inside her mouth gently before intertwining his tongue with hers.

Suddenly he stopped and pushed her way firmly, muttering to self, "I need to do this right."

He brought his forehead next to hers and said, "This is my first date with you and I want to get it right."

Touched by his series of gestures, Gayatri snuggled up to him and said, "You have done more than enough. There is no need to go through so much trouble."

"But Italian is your favourite cuisine and I want to feed you with my own hands today. So indulge me," he said earnestly.

Looking incongruous in her mother's kitchen, Aaryan started the process – rolling up his sleeves, his face carved in concentration. Gayatri decided that she was going to confess her feelings for him by the end of the meal.

"Why don't you take out the cutlery while I put the pasta to boil and the chocolate to melt?" said Aaryan, falling into his natural boss mode.

Thinking that he was taking the cooking thing a bit too seriously, she decided to ruffle him up a bit.

She stretched to her full height to reach past him for the wine glasses kept on the higher shelf, deliberately brushing against him in the process. The electric currents sizzled through her and must have reached him because he looked up. One of his hands snaked up to touch her bared midriff, while the other hand held the ladle stirring the chocolate cube. As Gayatri lowered herself down carefully with the glasses in hand, she felt the abrasion of his shirt and the jeans against her skimpy clothes, leaving her in no doubt about his arousal. Without realising, Aaryan raised his ladle holding hand next to her face, making the hot chocolate drip on her neck. With a yelp, Gayatri placed the wine glasses on the kitchen counter and ran to the water faucet. Aaryan came running with the ice cube in his hand and cursed himself for being so careless. Blowing gently on her reddened skin, he rubbed the ice gently on the affected area.

"I am truly sorry," he apologised.

Irritated with his porcelain doll treatment, she said tartly, "I am fine and made of sterner stuff, not like your emancipated girlfriends."

"You sound jealous," he said taking a bit of the liquid chocolate on his finger.

"So let's test how strong you really are. If I hear a peep from your mouth, you lose," he murmured.

And then, he smeared the liquid on her cheek, licking it almost immediately. Gayatri squeaked involuntarily at his licking, but put her hand on her mouth immediately. She winced as he dipped his finger again in the scalding pot, but Aaryan seemed impervious to the heat as he chose the next body part to torture.

"I would love to put it on your lips, but I think they are too delicate and precious for this game," he said hoarsely.

Gayatri sagged against the kitchen slab as a fresh wave of arousal hit her. Moving her hair away from the back of her neck, he put the chocolate there and nibbled slowly, savouring the taste.

"If I don't do anything fast, not only will I lose the bet but will also turn into liquid form myself," she thought desperately.

She pulled away from his sinful mouth, "I thought this feast was for me, instead you are the one gorging away. It is my turn now."

He waited in anticipation as she smeared the hot liquid on his earlobe and sucked. He growled deep in his throat and tried to stop her.

She tut-tutted, "You are not allowed to react, remember?"

Next, she spread the hot liquid liberally on his palm and dug her teeth into it.

Aaryan tipped back his head, "No more of this wooing bit…" saying so he shut the gas and roughly threw the stuff on the kitchen counter to the floor.

He whispered dangerously, "Ooh no, you don't get to go away…enough of your games now," as she tried to wiggle away.

He scooped her in his arms and put her up on the slab.

Aaryan looked at her in all seriousness and said, "I was going to do this the gentlemanly way, but you are way too tempting. So let me ask you this straight up – will you be my girl, now and forever?"

Tears shimmering, Gayatri shook her head in affirmation as her hands came up to hug him.

"I haven't finished yet. You need to know that I am going to be the most possessive and jealous man. So no more of those love-sick puppies hanging around you. I am also very demanding, so you shall need to devote all your time to me, whether at work or outside…"

Laughing, she put her fingers on his lips and simply said, "I love you, Aaryan. You turned my life upside down and righted it again. You are mine to love, mine forever!"

★★★